THE MOUSE WATCH UNDERWATER

J. J. GILBERT

Disney • HYPERION   LOS ANGELES   NEW YORK

For Olivia

Text copyright © 2021 by Disney Enterprises, Inc.

First Hardcover Edition, May 2021
First Paperback Edition, October 2021

10 9 8 7 6 5 4 3 2 1
FAC-025438-21232
Printed in the United States of America

This book is set in 12-point Goudy Old Style/MT, Nexa Slab/Fontspring
Designed by Joann Hill

Library of Congress Cataloging-in-Publication Control Number for Hardcover:
2020005101
ISBN 978-1-368-06822-2
Visit www.DisneyBooks.com

SUSTAINABLE FORESTRY INITIATIVE

Certified Sourcing

www.sfiprogram.org
SFI-01054

The SFI label applies to the text stock

FOREWORD

This purrrr-ticular Mouse Watch adventure was told to me on a rainy night by Jarvis Slinktail. He showed up at my house soaking wet. As we talked by the fire, I suppose all that water pouring down outside must have reminded him of one of the most dangerous adventures he and Bernie Skampersky took upon themselves in their early days in the Mouse Watch.

Being an avid scholar of all Mouse Watch–related activities, I eagerly grabbed my notebook and scribbled down the entire tale. Of course, in order to keep Jarvis's energy up (storytelling is hard work), I made certain to have a tray of assorted cheeses and a big bottle of Tabasco sauce at the ready.

It is with great pleasure that I share with you, dear reader, another exciting adventure from the Mouse Watch, those intrepid mice that keep the world safe from danger and harm. Sit back, grab a piece of your favorite cheese, and "sub-merge" into this one-of-a-kind underwater adventure!

—J. J. Gilbert

Bernie Skampersky raced down the gleaming white corridor that led to the Secret Watcher International Subway System. She checked her watch. The display showed a cartoon version of herself running next to a countdown clock. The clock was synched with the S.W.I.S.S. station terminal.

Two minutes to the next train! she thought. *I'd better hustle!*

She doubled her speed, calling back to her fellow agent Jarvis Slinktail to try to keep up. Jarvis, in spite of being much taller than she was, preferred sitting behind a keyboard rather than doing anything physical whatsoever. The lanky rat was her best friend, and she noticed that his shock of blond hair bounced comically in his eyes as he huffed and puffed, trying to keep pace with her.

"Last one there is a R.A.T.S. agent!" Bernie shouted.

"Not . . . (huff) . . . fair!" Jarvis called back. "I had a . . . (puff) . . . huge breakfast! Cheddar-cheese waffles!"

Bernie chuckled. Jarvis's appetite was becoming legendary at Mouse Watch HQ. It had gotten so bad that the cafeteria mice had been known to panic and lock the cafeteria doors when they saw him coming.

Bernie was a short brown mouse with a haystack of blue hair and long eyelashes. Joining the Mouse Watch had been her dream, one that had actually come true when she'd been accepted to the elite band of agents six months ago.

As she ran, she noticed how much steadier her breathing had become and that her legs were much stronger than when she'd first joined up. With the rigorous training exercises she did every day, she was starting to gain athletic abilities she'd never known, and clad in her official Level One agent uniform, a black jumpsuit with silver trim, she looked every bit a part of the illustrious team.

Bernie ran toward the secret area indicated on the map on her goggles' screen. The smart goggles were one of the Watchers' most important instruments, a hi-tech piece of enhanced-reality gear that allowed an agent to do countless useful things, including, as Bernie was using it for right then, consulting a highly accurate mapping system. She'd only used the S.W.I.S.S. station once before, and because Mouse Watch HQ was such a vast, sprawling warren of glass windows and mazelike corridors, the map was quite helpful.

She scurried past the locker room that led to the gym and reached the drinking fountains well before Jarvis did. By the time he caught up, she remembered to use the switch behind the fountains to open the secret door.

"What took you so long?" asked Bernie.

Jarvis was huffing and puffing so hard that he couldn't answer for a full thirty seconds. "T- . . . too . . ."

"Too? Too what?" asked Bernie. "Too far to run?"

"Too . . . basco sauce," wheezed Jarvis. "I forgot to grab some on the way out. Just give me a second to run back. . . ."

"No time!" Bernie cried. "We're on a schedule! Somebody needs rescuing and we have to go!"

Jarvis shrugged and held out his paws in a helpless gesture. "What if I need a snack? Nothing tastes good without Tabasco anymore!" he exclaimed. "I even put it on my cereal this morning!"

"You have a problem," said Bernie. "Come on, someone's in serious danger!"

The secret door behind the drinking fountains led to a very old stairway in a crumbling, brick-lined tunnel. Bernie found it interesting because it was very unlike the rest of the conspicuously clean, futuristic Mouse Watch headquarters. She had no idea what the old tunnel had been used for originally. But, seeing how ancient and crumbly the bricks were, Bernie wondered if it was part of a much older building that had once stood where HQ now was. Apparently, sometime in the distant past of Los Angeles, someone had needed a stairway to access the old tunnels beneath the city.

It was very mysterious.

But Bernie liked to imagine that a secret society used to meet there, making plans to take over the world, or that it was possibly a hideout for robbers while they plotted some kind of bank heist.

It was impossible for her not to feel daring and adventurous when descending the rickety stairs.

When she reached the bottom, Bernie checked her watch and was happy to see that they'd actually arrived with two seconds to spare. Despite the Tabasco-related slowdown, their training was paying off.

Grinning, she showed Jarvis her record time. The lanky rat nodded but looked wholly unimpressed. "Good for you," he said, sounding tired.

"If you put as much effort into physical training as you do into eating, next time we can make even better time," said Bernie.

"No thank you," said Jarvis. "Running through obstacle courses—"

"Is a fun challenge?" finished Bernie, grinning.

"No," said Jarvis. "I was gonna say, 'is my least favorite thing in the world to do.' Besides," he added, glancing at her through his blond mop of hair, "I say anybody who wastes their time running around when they could be thinking or playing video games has a misplaced set of priorities."

Jarvis was brilliant with computers. Bernie was good at solving puzzles, but there had never been, in Mouse Watch history, anybody better at it than Jarvis. He was the most natural code breaker the Watch had ever seen. They'd made an exception for him to join up with them, in spite of the fact that he was a rat and had once (even though he hadn't wanted to) worked for R.A.T.S.—the Rogue Animal Thieves Society.

The group had a dark reputation. They knew how to take advantage of every angle, how to manipulate and exploit anybody who was weak and vulnerable. Jarvis had needed help and they'd offered to take care of him . . . for a price. R.A.T.S. was the most corrupt gang of evildoers ever assembled, and they worked tirelessly for their own selfish purposes.

That included destroying anybody who stood in their way.

R.A.T.S.—which was made up of more than just rats, including assorted other villainous vermin and sneaky reptiles—was the archnemesis of the Mouse Watch. The evil, covert group sought to destroy the Mouse Watch and take the world back from humans. Bernie shuddered, thinking of the last time she'd gone up against R.A.T.S., when they had taken over New York City and tried to drive all humans underground. If not for the intrepid Mouse Watch, Bernie felt sure that there wouldn't have been anyone left to stop their diabolical deeds.

Bernie's goggles lit up with a blue glow that cast an eerie light in the dim shadows. A series of pop-up balloons appeared in the corner of the screen with instructions for how to use the transport system.

STEP ONE: SUMMON TRAIN USING VOICE COMMAND "HEY, S.W.I.S.S."

STEP TWO: STATE DESTINATION.

STEP THREE: AFTER BOARDING THE TRAIN, SELECT SPECIFIC DESTINATION FROM THE MENU.

STEP FOUR: BUCKLE UP!

Loudly and clearly, Bernie said, "Hey, S.W.I.S.S.!"

An electronic female voice with a light British accent replied, "Coming!"

A few seconds later, the shiny white Maglev train slid soundlessly up to the station platform. As she watched it approach, Bernie thought about her last adventure. At that time, she'd had a strong prejudice against rats. When she was just a mouseling, she'd had a run-in with one named Dr. Thornpaw, a horrible villain who had outfitted himself with powerful robotic limbs to replace the ones human scientists had ruined through tests and experiments. The soulless Dr. Thornpaw had taken her brother Brody's life, and it had haunted Bernie ever since. But that wasn't the last time she saw Dr. Thornpaw—she encountered him again on her first day as a Mouse Watch agent. The evil doctor had vowed revenge on all of humanity, and he also turned out to be one of the most formidable opponents the Mouse Watch had ever faced. The mind-controlling cheese spray he'd developed had nearly taken down New York City, turning all the citizens into zombies. Thanks to Bernie and Jarvis, he'd been stopped in his tracks and was now safely behind bars.

Not bad for a couple of rookies! thought Bernie, smiling.

It really was an understatement. She hadn't trusted Jarvis at first, but all of Bernie's preconceived notions about rats had disappeared when he saved her and a team of Mouse Watch agents from a deadly maze in Dr. Thornpaw's lab. Ever since, they'd been best friends.

The doors whooshed open, and Bernie and Jarvis boarded the S.W.I.S.S. She couldn't help but notice that Jarvis looked particularly uneasy. His whiskers drooped and his furry complexion was pale. The first time he'd ridden the supersonic train he'd gotten violently sick. She felt a wave of concern.

"Hey, did you bring some of those . . ." Bernie began.

"Motion-sickness tablets that Gadget designed?" finished Jarvis. "Yeah. Right here."

Jarvis pulled one of the tablets out of his pocket and popped it in his mouth. "At least it tastes like Tabasco-covered cheese," he said, chewing. "That's about the only good thing I can think of when riding this stupid train."

He raised the hood on his uniform and retreated within it like a turtle going into its shell. Jarvis's uniform matched Bernie's except for that necessary addition. Jarvis loved hoods, and the Watch had kindly customized his jumpsuit to accommodate his favorite accessory.

The two Watchers found their seats, stowed their backpacks beneath them, and secured their safety harnesses. The electronic female voice said, "Please state your destination."

"Portland, Oregon," said Bernie.

"Portland station," replied the S.W.I.S.S. "Please be sure your restraints are properly fastened. Arrival time, T minus three minutes, twenty-six seconds."

Bernie and Jarvis had barely fastened the buckles on their harnesses when, with a sonic *BOOM!* the train shot down the tracks like a bullet from a gun.

As the mouse-size train flew down the rails, navigating old sewer tunnels that intersected with the Watch's specially constructed new ones, Bernie thought of how different her current reality was compared to her old one.

Back in Thousand Acorns, her hometown, mice had to make the most out of everyday objects. For example, a thimble might make a good bowl for soup. A bottle cap could be an end table. And just about anything that could be salvaged from a toy store or a fashion doll's wardrobe could be reimagined or altered to fit a mouse. It was creative but always just a little bit uncomfortable.

Now that she was an agent at the Mouse Watch, she enjoyed all kinds of new, mouse-size comforts and devices. This was definitely thanks to Gadget Hackwrench, the head inventor and leader of the organization. Gadget was a legend from her days working with Chip and Dale's Rescue Rangers, and Bernie had studied everything there was to know about her hero, including her early inventions, like the Ranger Plane.

Since breaking off from the Rescue Rangers and starting her own organization, Gadget had progressed with the times and had turned her genius brain to developing the amazing tiny tech and miniature comforts that the Mouse Watch now relied upon. Bernie never knew how great life could be until she'd become a Watcher. She was living the dream, even though her new life was also filled with danger.

But for her, danger added a little spice.

Not so much for Jarvis. The only spice he craved could be found in a small bottle of hot sauce.

That, and solving a good puzzle.

As if on cue, Bernie's watch pinged, alerting her that the timetable for her rescue operation was ticking away. When on a mission, the smart watch counted down rather than up, and she noticed that she only had thirty minutes to complete the task.

She felt nervous. Bernie had no idea who they were going to rescue, but she knew that it must have been a really important mission to have such a short and urgent countdown to get there. A thirty-minute rescue meant that it was a top priority. Someone was most certainly in immediate danger.

Well, they assigned the right rodents to the job, Bernie thought. She and Jarvis were both eager to prove themselves.

Even though the S.W.I.S.S. was incredibly fast, Bernie couldn't help but wish it could go even faster. Every agent would be evaluated on their mission performance and, although she'd never been a stellar student in school back home, here at the Mouse Watch she was determined to get top marks as a Level One recruit.

Almost as quickly as it had begun, the train ride was ending. Bernie reached for the straps of her backpack as the train slowed, anxious to bolt out of the doors and get to the address on her smart watch display.

"Mount Tabor Park," she murmured. The watch showed that the Portland neighborhood was about twenty minutes from the Portland Mouse Watch terminal. In order to get there on time they were going to have to really move.

"Better get your Pop! Cycle ready, Jarvie," said Bernie. "We've got a race ahead of us. . . ."

"Do you really have to call me that?" mumbled Jarvis. "It sounds so babyish."

Bernie glanced over to Jarvis, who was slouching in his seat, arms folded across his chest and his hoodie pulled low over his eyes.

"Jar?"

"Mmmgh," said Jarvis.

Bernie pulled back his hood so she could see his face. The skinny rat stared at her with his big brown eyes. Bernie could tell that, in spite of the motion sickness pills, he looked a little queasy.

"You okay?" asked Bernie.

"Ugh," said Jarvis, sitting up. "I hate these stupid trains. Why couldn't Gadget invent some kind of dematerializing transport device, one that would go BRZZZT! and your atomic particles would be immediately reassembled wherever you wanted to go?"

"I'm no scientist, but turning yourself into a bunch

of random particles sounds like a bad idea," said Bernie. "Although, if anybody could figure out how to do it, Gadget could. Hey, I've got some water in my backpack. You can drink it if you think it will help settle your stomach."

Jarvis shook his head and motioned her away. "Thanks, but I'll be okay. Just get me back on solid ground."

Bernie felt the train glide to a stop as it approached the Portland terminal, and a few seconds later the door slid open and the voice said, "Arrived. Please disembark."

Without hesitation, Jarvis grabbed his backpack and they both rushed out the door. Unlike New York's Grand Central Terminal platform, the Portland stop was a very simple affair, just a brick platform beneath a manhole cover. Bernie spotted a mouse-size iron ladder that had been installed next to a small doorway.

She checked her watch. "We've only got eighteen minutes! Hurry!"

"Seriously, Bern," groused Jarvis. "How does the S.W.I.S.S. not affect you at ALL?"

"I have a very sturdy constitution. I think it may be part of why I got recruited."

It was true. Bernie was small, but she was mighty. Nothing kept her down for long. Even a broken leg hadn't stopped her from traveling all the way to the Mouse Watch headquarters for her first day on the job.

Bernie led the way, scrambling up the tiny ladder and emerging through the door into an old back alley. Outside, the fall weather felt cool and crisp. The sky was dotted with a few dark clouds, but between them, the late-afternoon sun shone through. According to the map in her goggles' display, they'd emerged at a spot near the Hawthorne Bridge, a spectacular truss bridge that spanned the massive Willamette River.

The sun's fading rays sparkled on the water, dazzling their eyes. If they'd had the time, Bernie would have loved to scamper along the banks of the river with Jarvis and maybe find a spot for a picnic—hidden away from human eyes, of course. In that brief daydream, Bernie would have brought plenty of Tabasco sauce, and she and Jarvis would have spent a lovely afternoon joking and laughing as the sun went down.

It was a beautiful thought. But there was no time for goofing around. Someone important was in serious danger.

"Let's ride," said Bernie, lowering her goggles. "We're—"

"Burning daylight. I know," finished Jarvis.

With a practiced motion, they reached into their nylon backpacks and retrieved aluminum cylinders, which snapped apart with a *POP!* A gleaming, futuristic-looking pod shot out from each tube, unfolding automatically into a mouse-size motorcycle.

Bernie never got tired of Gadget's tech. It was like magic. Her boss really was amazing.

VROOOAOOWWW! Bernie hit the gas hard with her hind paw, and the engine revved into gear. The map to Mount Tabor appeared on her goggles as she rocketed down the scenic Portland city streets, sticking to shadows cast by the curbs. Jarvis followed close behind.

Bernie watched the countdown clock in the corner of her screen and winced. This one was gonna be close!

She increased her speed. Bernie knew that anyone who might have been looking in their direction would have seen two very tiny figures weaving in and out of gutters and next to sidewalk curbs, avoiding random pieces of litter and the occasional pothole or crack. They would have perhaps mistaken the two small riders for a couple of normal, if fast-moving, rodents, or exceptionally large low-flying insects. Bernie knew that only the most observant among the humans would have been amazed to see that they were really a mouse and a rat, each clothed in tiny jumpsuits, rocketing down the street on custom high-tech motorcycles.

Gadget had taught them that, as a rule, humans tended to ignore the unusual because it was easier to believe what fit neatly into their worldview.

Crime-fighting rodents did not fit into most people's worldview.

This was an advantage for every Watcher.

The Mouse Watch always tried to hide its activities from human eyes as much as possible, and this human tendency toward denial worked to their benefit. It helped them to get from place to place in public while avoiding detection.

As Bernie and her best friend sped to their target, hoping beyond hope that they wouldn't be too late, she wondered what the mission would be. They hadn't been told exactly *who* they were rescuing or from *what*, but it had to be important if they'd been directed to drop everything to get there so quickly.

To calm her nerves as she raced along, she recited the Mouse Watch creed to herself:

Every part of a watch is important, from the smallest gear on up. For without each part working together, keeping time is impossible. We never sleep. We never fail. We are there for all who call upon us in their time of need. We are the MOUSE WATCH!

And with the inspirational thought of those very special words, words that meant everything to her, Bernie took courage and raced on into the gathering darkness, anxious to get to their destination before time ran out.

CHAPTER 2

When Bernie and Jarvis screeched to a stop at the address indicated on their enhanced reality goggles, a quiet tree-lined street, neither of them knew what they were supposed to do right away. The green dot that indicated their target glowed steadily. But the street was deserted, and no other information was forthcoming.

"The GPS says whoever needs us is right here," said Bernie. "Why can't I see them?" Bernie leapt from her Pop! Cycle and stared around wildly. "Hello? We're here to help!" she shouted.

Jarvis squinted up and down the street and threw his arms up. "I have no idea!" He and Bernie both looked around, then, at the same time, they looked at the street beneath their feet. "Is it . . . under us?" Jarvis asked.

"A subterranean rescue!" said Bernie excitedly.

"Or maybe the target is wearing an invisibility suit?"

They both waved their arms around, hoping to bump into something solid. But they had no luck.

"This is weird," said Bernie. "I don't get it."

"What if we check the roofs? That house over there with the Halloween decorations looks suspicious," said Jarvis, eyeing a roof display of large rubber rats with red eyes and huge fangs.

"I don't think we were sent here to rescue a bunch of rubber rodents," said Bernie.

"Yeah, I guess you're right. I just don't see—"

"Meow."

The tiny sound made them both suddenly freeze in their tracks.

"Wait! Look there!" said Jarvis.

"Where?" replied Bernie.

"Up there!" Jarvis was pointing up, into the branches of the maple tree right in front of them.

Bernie squinted through her goggles. The device, reading the movement of her eyes, automatically zoomed in on the direction she was looking. But when Bernie spotted the target, her tail went rigid.

"A cat!" she squeaked. "We're rescuing a *cat*?"

A tiny gray ball of fur peeked out at them from among the branches.

"It's just a kitten," Jarvis said, breaking into a smile.

"Aww, it's so cute! Poor thing, it must be so scared stuck all the way up there in that tree."

"Cute? *Scared?* It's a cat. A little one, but still, a CAT!" said Bernie.

"But just look at it. Look at its little paws!" said Jarvis. "Hang on, I'm gonna take a picture and post it on Instagouda!"

Bernie stared at him in shock. For her entire life she'd been taught about the dangers of cats. Back in Thousand Acorns, an alarm system of cleverly hidden strings with bells on them ran throughout the neighborhood, alerting residents instantly to any cat who accidentally tripped them. These were called Fee-lines, and Bernie had always been grateful that they were there.

Kittens grow up to be cats, thought Bernie. *And cats eat mice.* Even a kitten, given the chance, might try to attack a mouse. It might have been cute, but it was a predator!

"Okay, no way. I don't want to do this," huffed Bernie, raising her goggles. "I can't believe we raced all the way over here for a cat."

"It needs our help," said Jarvis, shrugging.

Bernie turned to Jarvis and shook her head, exasperated. "I thought we'd be rescuing a human or a mouse. This is helping the enemy!"

Jarvis was still looking at the stranded kitten through his goggles. "You thought I was the enemy once, just because

I was a rat. Come on, Bernie, let's give it a chance! It's just a kitten! Besides, not all cats are bad. I met one once that was a vegetarian!"

Bernie let out a disbelieving snort. "Right."

"It was. It loved pea soup with carrots," Jarvis said obstinately, ignoring her as he reached into his pack and removed a large plastic case.

"Do we really have to do this?" asked Bernie, wringing her paws.

"You know we do," said Jarvis. "Those are the directions."

Bernie knew that the Mouse Watch law was to help any creature who was in need. It was the core principle that every recruit agreed to upon signing up.

But it didn't mean she had to like it.

With an exasperated sigh, Bernie removed the other half of the rescue device she'd been carrying in her own backpack and, within a few seconds, she and Jarvis had assembled the two halves to a portable drone, one that Gadget had designed for rescuing small animals caught in precarious places. It was equipped with a retractable net, and the engine that powered it was especially strong, able to lift creatures many times its own weight.

"Hey, I just thought of a good name for this thing," said Jarvis. "A *Kitty CAT-cher*. Get it? Kitty cat? Catch? Pretty good, right?"

Bernie rolled her eyes. "I think Gadget's name, the

S.A.R.D.-ine, Small Animal Rescue Drone, is just fine," she said. Suddenly, a thought occurred to her. If she was instrumental in pulling off this rescue, even if it was a cat, she might get extra points on her mission review. She cared more about that than her conviction that all cats were bad.

Bernie really wanted to advance to Level Two as quickly as possible.

She'd hoped that after proving herself in New York, she and Jarvis would be able to get out of the mundane things that most new recruits had to do and skip right to the big, important stuff. It was rare for a couple of brand-new recruits to go head-to-head with a supervillain, save the Mouse Watch, *and* free an entire city from the clutches of a cheese-scented mind-control spray, all on their first day on the job. But unfortunately, Gadget Hackwrench had insisted that basic training was necessary for every new recruit.

And Bernie wanted it to be over with just as soon as possible.

Once she was promoted to Level Two, she could get back to going on important missions. Rescuing a cat was hardly a saving-the-world situation. But if she could get a stellar review on this simple task, it might mean she was one step closer to fighting supervillains again.

"Hey, Jarvie, mind if I work the controls?" Bernie asked.

"I thought we decided on 'Jar,'" he said. Then Jarvis

glanced over and raised an eyebrow at her. "Have you ever worked one of these before? Drones are tricky."

"How hard can it be?" asked Bernie lightly. She reached for the touch-screen controller. Jarvis hesitated before turning it over.

"Hard," he said. "The first time I flew one I totally crashed it." He glanced worriedly at the helpless cat. "We can't afford to risk the life of that kitten. What if you messed up? If that little guy got hurt, you'd never forgive yourself!" He paused, seeming to remember Bernie's aversion to cats. "At least, *I* wouldn't."

Bernie had a good heart, but she could also be impulsive and headstrong. When she was growing up, her parents had told her a thousand times to "just stop and think first!"

She tended to ignore that piece of constructive criticism.

And sure, she knew that thinking first wasn't her strong suit. But she trusted her instincts. And at that moment the need to succeed at the mission, to distinguish herself in front of her hero Gadget and maybe even Chip and Dale, too, overcame any common sense.

"I know how to work it. I've done a simulation. Please, Jar . . ."

She could tell by Jarvis's expression that he thought it was a bad idea. But Bernie knew that her best friend also had a soft spot when it came to her begging, and that he usually couldn't resist when she really wanted to do something. The lanky rat reluctantly handed her the controls.

"Okay, fine, but you have to let me give you advice. If it starts to go bad, I'm grabbing it back, 'kay? Don't fight me on it."

"Yeah, sure," Bernie said quickly. "Hand it over!"

The truth was that she had done a drone-simulation app once during training, and she had almost landed the drone successfully.

Almost.

Not my fault. Probably just a glitch. They really need to design a better app, she'd convinced herself when she'd gotten a failing score.

She was a very resourceful mouse. She'd beaten the odds just to get an invite to the Mouse Watch in the first place.

She could do this.

WHIRRRRR! The propeller blades spun as the drone lifted into the air. Bernie watched the screen carefully, trying to be certain that the pitch axis on the propeller blades stayed even.

"So far, so good," murmured Jarvis. "No sudden moves. Just keep it steady."

Bernie was only half listening. She was completely immersed in the digital map on the touch screen, watching it closely as the machine neared the top of the maple tree.

A light on the screen flashed and text appeared: *Enable Autopilot?*

"Okay, Bernie, you should definitely enable the auto function," said Jarvis.

Bernie shook her head. "I can do it manually," she said.

"Dude, no!" said Jarvis. "You need more training. I'm telling you, engage the autopilot! There's no room for error."

"I've got this," said Bernie confidently, edging the virtual joystick forward to navigate among the branches of the big maple. It still bothered her that Jarvis had passed his drone pilot exam with flying colors and that she'd completely bombed. But this was her chance to get it right. She needed to prove to herself that she could do this! She could see the kitten in the drone's camera looking anxious as the vehicle approached.

"Watch out for that branch!" said Jarvis.

Bernie swooped below it at the last second, the blades of the drone shearing off a couple of maple leaves as it narrowly missed the branch.

"Here, let me have it back," said Jarvis nervously.

"Stop worrying! I said I've got it!" said Bernie.

"Bernie!"

"No!"

She edged the drone closer to the cat. Secretly, she was very pleased with herself. This was going even better than expected! As the drone drew close, the nervous kitten edged back toward the trunk of the tree, caught between the frightening machine and a deadly drop far below.

Another text message appeared on the screen. *Deploy Catnip Lure?*

Bernie tapped the "Y" button. A net dropped from the bottom of the drone, just as a hidden jet released a small spray of liquid catnip. The kitten's eyes widened. Catnip was the only thing that could make it forget the scary situation it was in. The cute, furry little creature bounded forward directly into the center of the net and started rolling around playfully.

"Gotcha!" said Bernie triumphantly as she levitated the drone upward, carrying the surprised kitten with it. "See? I told you I had this. You need to have more faith in other critters, Jar. You worry too mu—"

But Bernie didn't finish her speech. She wasn't watching the screen closely enough and missed seeing a branch creeping up on the side of the drone.

CRAWWWWUNCH!

"Pull up, pull up!" shouted Jarvis.

"Rowwwww!" wailed the kitten.

Bernie tried to regain control of the drone as it spun and twirled erratically, bouncing violently off the tree branches like a pinball in a pinball machine.

"MEOOOWWW!" yowled the kitty.

"Aaaah!" shouted Jarvis.

Panicking, Bernie gunned the throttle forward and, with the kitten swinging crazily beneath it, the drone shot out of the tree and rocketed straight toward the house.

"Bernie! Slow down!" Jarvis cried. "You're gonna crash! Give me the controls!"

"I'll save him!" shouted Bernie, sliding her paws over the touch-screen controls.

She'd just managed to stop the drone from hitting the house and was maneuvering it lower to the ground when her paw slipped, causing the drone to suddenly flip upside down! The kitten let out a terrified screech as it hung from the net with one claw. There was a split-second moment of terror. Then, horror of horrors, Bernie watched as the tiny kitten tumbled from the net!

"AAAAHH!" cried Jarvis.

Bernie had never seen the rat move more quickly in her entire life. Until that moment, she didn't know if Jarvis had any muscles in his entire lanky frame—except the well-developed jaw muscles he used for chewing!

But as the kitten tumbled down, Jarvis, with arms extended, raced to catch it. The heroic rat slid beneath it just in time, cushioning the much larger animal's fall.

"Ow," said a voice from under the meowing ball of fur.

"Jarvis! Jarvis! Are you okay?" screamed Bernie as she raced over to her friend. The kitten was terrified but all right. As it stood up on shaky paws, Bernie could see that Jarvis was all right, too. A little squashed, but all right.

"Oof. Th- . . . that was . . ." he began shakily.

". . . wild!" finished Bernie. "And impressive! You were like a superhero! I've never seen you move so fast!"

Jarvis grinned sheepishly and quivered a little as he rose up from the ground. "That kitten may be cute, but it's *heavy*!" Then, remembering why the near tragedy had just happened, he shot Bernie an annoyed look and said, "Next time . . ."

Bernie knew where he was going and nodded quickly, ". . . it's all yours. I'm not touching another drone until I have more training."

Jarvis seemed satisfied with her response. Glancing over at the mewing, confused kitten, he said, "Okay, so, now that the little guy is safe and sound, what do we do? We can't just leave him here."

Bernie glanced at the house. "And we don't want the humans to know we're here either." She gazed around the yard and then noticed a small basket filled with a towel and sprinkler toys near the front door.

"I've got an idea," she said, grinning.

After emptying the big basket of its contents, they struggled to pull it over to the doorstep. Then with even more grunting and straining, Bernie and Jarvis hoisted the mewing baby cat into the basket and covered it with a towel. To Bernie, the kitten looked a lot like a baby being left on a doorstep. The little creature seemed very content to stay there rather than to attempt climbing a tree again.

Bernie pounded on the door as loudly as she could, but because she was so tiny it hardly made a sound at all.

"We need to let the owner know their cat is safe!" said Bernie.

"How about we throw one of these at it?" asked Jarvis, pointing at a pile of matchbox-size racer cars on the side of the porch.

"Good idea," said Bernie. She and Jarvis each grabbed an end of a small green Corvette.

"Ready? One . . . Two . . . THREE!"

On "three" they tossed the little car as hard as they could against the front door. It wasn't a loud sound, but it was enough to set a small dog barking inside the house, and a second or two later she heard a muffled human voice call, "Coming!"

Bernie and Jarvis shared a quick glance, then scrambled underneath a nearby mulberry bush. From their hiding spot, they watched as a kindly-looking old woman answered the door, then looked down to see the kitten staring up at her with big, innocent eyes.

"Now how in the world did you get in there?" asked the woman with a chuckle.

When the old lady had taken the mewing kitten in her

arms and gone back inside, Bernie and Jarvis scampered across the lawn to retrieve the drone. Bernie shook her head in frustration as she stopped the timer on her smart watch. The entire operation had gone ten minutes over the time limit. Not only had she botched the low-level mission, but the missed deadline would be noted in a report.

I really don't want to see Alph's face when we get back, thought Bernie. *She's going to be disappointed.*

The head mouse in charge of new recruits had been Bernie's first friend in the Mouse Watch, but she was tough!

After separating the drone and storing it into their packs, the two mice gunned their Pop! Cycles and headed back to the S.W.I.S.S. station. The air rushed through Bernie's whiskers as they rode. The cool Portland air smelled wonderful, redolent with the scent of pine and an approaching rainstorm. Unfortunately, right then Bernie couldn't really appreciate it. She wanted to forget this less than stellar performance.

"I really do hate cats, even if that one was kind of cute," groused Bernie into the wind as her motorcycle shot down the damp, leaf-strewn street. Enough of this low-level stuff. What she really wanted was to do something important. A top-level mission. Hadn't she and Jarvis defeated Thornpaw? Neutralizing a foe of that caliber was far more important than a kitten rescue, wasn't it?

When I get back to HQ, I'm going to make a formal

request, Bernie thought. *I'll make them assign us something big. Something important.*

But inwardly she wondered how that would be possible if they couldn't get a simple kitten rescue done on time.

She sighed, feeling discouraged. The wind, growing damp and cooler now that the sun had gone down, whistled around her as she sped along the darkening Portland streets.

CHAPTER 3

"Ten minutes over? Could have been better, Rook," said Alph, consulting a mouse-size digital tablet. The pretty, red-haired mouse was Bernie's and Jarvis's immediate supervisor. Bernie liked Alph and respected her a lot. But, as Bernie feared, she hadn't responded well to the request that Bernie and Jarvis be sent on more important missions.

"Yeah, I know, but seriously, Alph, a kitten rescue? Come on! Jarvie and I saved New York City from the worst baddie you guys have ever encountered!" said Bernie.

"Don't call me Jarvie!" hissed the rat, flushing crimson with embarrassment in front of his boss.

"That was a special circumstance," said Alph, her hands firmly on her hips. "Right now you and Jarvie are only Level One. That means that you do all the basic missions until—"

Her lecture was interrupted by a loud, beeping alarm. Bernie and Jarvis glanced up, listening closely for further instructions.

A hologram of Gadget accompanied by Chip and Dale appeared in Alph's office, materializing on her cluttered desk. Bernie knew that an identical hologram was also appearing at the same time to the other agents all over HQ. This was not a personal visit or call. The alarm meant that something important needed to be communicated to all agents at once.

"Greetings, Watchers," said Gadget. Bernie noticed that she was clad in her usual lavender jumpsuit and had her smart goggles perched on top of her head. Her expression was serious. It was strange to see all three of the Rescue Ranger legends' normally chipper faces looking so alarmed.

"There's been an attack on our London base by a large number of R.A.T.S. operatives. They've come in with heavy artillery; some of our British friends have mentioned significant quantities of superglue traps and peanut butter bombs. Our London agents have lost one of their main structures as a result. All agents Level Two and above are instructed to leave via S.W.I.S.S. immediately and join me there. Chip and Dale will oversee the agents left behind. Gadget out!"

The hologram vanished. Bernie and Jarvis exchanged meaningful glances. The expression on Bernie's face was one of anger and disappointment. Why only Level Two and above? She would have loved to go on a mission exactly like this one!

But the expression on Jarvis's face was one of mild relief. He seemed much more ready to stay back and keep working on his lessons before taking on too many risks.

"Wow, well, that means I'm going to have to turn you two over to Chip and Dale," said Alph. "Since you are the only Level One agents in training right now, I'm sure the chipmunks will have instructions for you when they arrive." She glanced at her smart watch. "Yikes! I have to go. Duty calls!"

She gave Bernie and Jarvis a quick salute and dashed out of the room.

"Is it me, or does this feel like déjà vu?" asked Jarvis.

Bernie thought back to their last big mission. At the time they'd been training in a VR simulation and had emerged from it to find every agent gone. It had turned out that all the Los Angeles agents had been kidnapped by Thornpaw and his lab rats. Bernie and Jarvis had been on their own.

In a way, the situation in which they now found themselves didn't feel that much different, except this time they were being left with chaperones.

"Hey, Jarvie?" said Bernie.

"Huh?" said Jarvis.

"Sorry for trying to take the controls and screwing up the mission." Bernie reached into her pocket and handed him a small wrapped package.

He smiled at her. "Bern, this is totally unnecessary."

"Yeah, I know, I know," said Bernie. "Open it."

Jarvis unwrapped the small gift and grinned happily at what he found. "Hey, a Lazer Blazer! Cool!"

"It has a ton of features. Laser pointer, laser blaster, laser scanner . . ."

"Oh yeah, I know all about these from the Sharper Rodent catalog," enthused Jarvis. "It's a supercool gadget. I was hoping to get one with my next paycheck. Thanks!" He gave her a half hug and Bernie grinned happily. She loved seeing how interesting little gadgets made her friend so happy.

The gift had been expensive, and Bernie had been planning on saving it for Jarvis's birthday. To buy it, Bernie had sold one of her favorite Gadget Hackwrench collectibles on EekBay. She didn't regret giving it to him early. It was worth every penny to see his excitement over the new present.

The door at the back of Alph's office burst open and two very familiar figures entered, looking rushed and harried. Chip's fedora was tilted askew, and Dale's fur looked like it hadn't been combed in a week.

"Slinktail and Skampersky?" asked Chip in his quick, high-pitched voice.

"That's us!" said Bernie. She tried to sound confident, but inside she was geeking out. She was meeting Chip and Dale in person for the first time! The Rescue Rangers were legends in their own right, and, if Bernie had allowed herself, she would have been almost as starstruck around them as she was the first time she'd met Gadget.

Dale motioned for them to follow. Smiling broadly in anticipation, Bernie dashed after the Rescue Rangers with Jarvis in tow. Whatever they were going to be assigned had to be better than rescuing a kitten. In fact, just seeing that Chip and Dale were in charge made Bernie think that maybe, just maybe, her wish for something more important to do might actually come true.

They followed Chip and Dale to the zoom chutes, a network of massive transparent tubes that transported the Watchers all over the building using high-powered vacuum suction.

As they approached the opening, Bernie heard the familiar roar of churning air behind the thin glass door. She grinned in anticipation. She loved shooting around inside the tubes at a mile a minute, screaming her head off. It was like the best roller coaster in the world!

Of course, one glance at Jarvis told Bernie that he felt

exactly the opposite. He was gulping and muttering darkly about "serious concerns" and saying "bad for the appetite" as he followed the chipmunks to the entrance.

Chip placed his paw on the touch screen positioned outside the transport, and the door slid open with a loud *WHOOOSH!* Seconds later, Bernie found herself sucked right into the tunnel and flying through the tubes faster than a speeding bullet.

"WHOOO-HOOO!" she shouted. Through the transparent tubes, various rooms in Mouse Watch HQ sped past her in a colorful blur. Her whiskers were plastered against the sides of her cheeks and her ears stuck out straight behind her head, blown back by the tremendous force.

Usually, a trip to another room in HQ took only a matter of a few seconds. But Bernie realized, with a start, that she'd been in the tube well over thirty seconds and that there was no sign of it stopping.

What's going on? she wondered. *Is the machine malfunctioning?*

The world outside the transparent tubes grew suddenly dark as she felt them tilt sharply downward, plunging directly underground.

We must be traveling to a part of Mouse Watch HQ that I've never seen before!

In the six months since her arrival, she'd made a point

of exploring every nook and cranny she could find, often bursting by accident into more than a few top secret meetings held in private conference rooms.

But the place Chip and Dale were leading her to was apparently so well hidden, she wouldn't have found it in a million years.

"Accessing station Juliet Alpha Sierra," said an electronic voice. Bernie noticed, as she was flying down the tube, that the voice was very different from the one at the S.W.I.S.S. transport. The voice was low and male and almost whispered the information.

A tingle of excitement shot through her. *I've never heard that before*, she thought.

She wondered why they hadn't taken the S.W.I.S.S. It seemed to her that if they were going to travel a long distance, then the Maglev train would have been the most efficient way to go.

But, then again, maybe this is something different, she thought. Judging from the secret coordinates, perhaps it led to some top secret destination that most of the other agents didn't know about.

That thought made her whiskers vibrate with excitement.

When they arrived at their destination, Bernie hopped out of the bottom of the zoom chute and immediately noticed the briny smell of sea air. She gazed around at the huge, cathedral-like building that she found herself in. Gigantic windows stretched high above the old brick walls, illuminating swarms of dust motes that traveled down rays of light to a massive cement floor. An assortment of human-size oars, rowboats, and old ship-building equipment towered over them. It looked like an old boat workshop for humans.

And there, through the windows, Bernie saw the ocean.

Bernie had never seen the ocean!

Jarvis gasped. At first, Bernie thought it was because he was impressed with the architecture, but she soon saw the real reason why. A mouse hole in the wall by the windows opened to a tiny moat, with a mouse-size indoor dock. Next to the dock was a battleship. To Bernie, it looked like something out of a World War II movie, except that it was perfectly scaled down to rodent size.

"Wow," said Bernie. "Check that out!"

Chip overheard her talking to Jarvis and turned to give her a wink. "This is a special facility," he said in his quick, clipped voice. "Top secret oceanographic missions only."

Then, as he and Dale led them toward the big gray battleship, Bernie turned to Jarvis and whispered, "Isn't this cool?"

But she stopped short when she saw the horrified look on Jarvis's face. "What is it?"

After a big gulp, Jarvis said, "I . . . I hope that we're not being assigned to some kind of water rescue."

"Why?" asked Bernie. "Do you have a problem with swimming?"

"No," said Jarvis shakily. "I have a problem with drowning!"

Bernie felt confused. "But I'd always heard that rats liked ships. What's the big deal?"

Jarvis closed his eyes tightly. "I fell into a full watering can when I was little. I never learned how to swim, and I nearly drowned. Ever since then, I've had nightmares about large bodies of water." He paused. "And small ones. Basically, all water scares me."

He stopped walking. After staring at the retreating forms of Chip and Dale for a moment, he glanced up at the massive battleship and shook his head vigorously.

"Nope, nope, nope! I can't do it. I'll see you back at HQ," he said firmly. As he turned to walk away, Bernie grabbed his arm, pulling him up short.

"You can't do that, Jar!" she hissed. "You'll be booted out of the Mouse Watch. We can't just refuse a mission because we're scared!"

Jarvis hesitated, a look of pure torture on his kind face. His muzzle twitched, and Bernie thought he looked like he might cry.

"Hey, it's okay, I'm right here with you," said Bernie

gently, patting his arm. "We don't even know if we have to go out to sea. Maybe we're just supposed to clean the ship or something?"

Jarvis stared down at her with his big brown eyes. Bernie could see in them the small flicker of hope that her words were giving him. "Come on," she said. "We can do this."

Jarvis glanced back at the ship. Then, after what seemed like a huge internal struggle, he nodded slowly and let out a big sigh.

"Fine. But don't judge me if I start freaking out, okay?" he said.

"I would never judge you, Jarvie," said Bernie. "You're my best friend. Now come on."

The two friends set out after the chipmunks and were soon boarding a long gangplank onto the deck of the ship.

"This is the first mouse-size seafaring vessel ever constructed," Chip said as they walked. "It was a remarkable feat of engineering when it was built in the 1940s. Of course, now we have more sophisticated technology, but try to imagine how impressive this was back then."

As she took in her surroundings, Bernie felt like she was stepping into a time capsule filled with Mouse Watch history.

But Jarvis looked like he was stepping into a nightmare.

CHAPTER 4

"Welcome to the *Stargazer*," said Dale, grinning broadly and displaying his two prominent buckteeth. "The human history books never mention it, but this ship was actually the reason the Allies won World War II." He gestured to the interior of the cockpit in which they all were standing.

Bernie looked around, appreciating the ancient technology. There was a vast assortment of old-fashioned dials, gauges, and big, square buttons that lit up in different colors all over the control panel. In the middle of the room was a big, thronelike chair where Bernie guessed the captain used to sit. She was about to ask who had commanded the ship when Dale spoke, as if reading her thoughts.

"It was in here that Commander Lilian Brie launched a stealth mission to recover a secret weapon that still remains secret to this day. And although that mission failed, the intel she gained while at sea was given to Winston Churchill, and it helped him break the Axis codes," continued Dale.

"What part of the mission failed?" asked Bernie, hoping it didn't have to do with the ship's ability to stay afloat.

"That information will be given in due time, Skampersky," said Chip. "We'd like you both to join us in the navigation room at eighteen hundred hours for a top secret briefing. In the meantime, feel free to stroll around the ship. You'll find that there have been temporary quarters arranged, but don't worry about your luggage. We've sent for it and it will arrive a bit later."

Dale chimed in, saying, "And, if you're hungry, the galley is open. I hear that they're making cheese fondue today! Mmmmmm!" He rubbed his belly over his Hawaiian shirt for emphasis.

Normally, Bernie would have expected a burst of enthusiasm from Jarvis at the mention of fondue. But to her surprise, her lanky friend said nothing. He just raised the hood of his uniform and shoved his paws deeper into his pockets.

"Thank you . . . both," said Bernie awkwardly. "I haven't had a chance to say what a pleasure it is getting to meet you. I've been a huge fan of yours and Gadget's for, well, all my life."

The chipmunks both beamed at her. "We've heard a

lot about you and your friend here, too," admitted Chip, grinning. "That was nice work you did back in New York. It's part of the reason why we asked for you on this mission. That's some good timing that all other agents are off on that urgent all-hands mission."

So we're not just going to be cleaning the ship! thought Bernie excitedly.

"How long is the mission?" asked Bernie.

"We've planned for a week, but it could be longer or shorter depending on how soon we meet our objective. We'll give you more info at the briefing."

"Sounds great!" she said. But Bernie's feelings of anticipation were tempered a little at the thought of her friend's apprehension about the ocean. She glanced at Jarvis, who seemed to have retreated farther into his hoodie so that just his flop of blond hair and the tip of his muzzle could be seen sticking out from under it.

Chip and Dale gave a quick salute and climbed down a ladder that led belowdecks, leaving Bernie and Jarvis alone.

"Hungry?" asked Bernie hopefully. Food always cheered up Jarvis. She reached into her jumpsuit pocket and pulled out a small bottle filled with dark red fluid. "Guess what I brought?" she said, shaking the little bottle of Tabasco sauce playfully in front of Jarvis's nose. "How 'bout we head over to the galley and spice up that hot-cheese dip?"

Jarvis didn't say anything. Bernie knew that he must be really anxious if Tabasco sauce didn't perk him up.

"Well, it's here if you want it," she said, glancing at her watch. "We have twenty minutes until the meeting. Might as well go exploring." She walked around the cockpit, marveling at the old-fashioned dials and controls and pointing them out to Jarvis. Ordinarily he would have been excited to examine the historic technology, but he barely acknowledged the gesture. "Hrmph," he mumbled, shrugging.

"Come on, let's check out the galley. You might get hungry once we're there."

Bernie led the way down the gray metal stairs with Jarvis in tow. At the bottom, the stairs led into a long hallway, and she followed the signs for the galley. Old black-and-white photographs lined the walls, showing mice in uniform from the 1940s. Most of them had long passed away, but in the photos they looked lively and filled with passion. It was somehow comforting to Bernie that they were there. They were reminders that the Mouse Watch was carrying out the legacy of heroic mice throughout history. She was part of a long line of heroes who were willing to risk their lives to do good for others.

They knew before they reached the last door that they had found the galley, because the warm, delicious aroma of melted cheese was wafting toward them. Bernie hazarded a glance at Jarvis and noticed the merest twitch of his nose.

Not his usual ravenous excitement, but it's a start, she reasoned.

Inside the room was a basic set of metal dining tables and chairs. Like the other furniture on the ship, they were also bolted securely to the floor. Probably to keep them from sliding around during stormy weather. She glanced at Jarvis, hoping he wasn't imagining the same thing.

Almost as soon as they sat down at one of the tables, a cheery voice said, "Welcome, young agents!" Out of the kitchen stepped a mouse wearing a bright orange chef's hat and a big, toothy smile. She was carrying an enormous red pot filled with melty cheese. "My name is Agent Melissa McScurrie, but you can just call me Mac if you want to. I'm the cook aboard the *Stargazer*, and it's my mission to add a homey feeling to this dreary ship," she said, smiling.

"Hi, Mac. I'm Bernie and this is Jarvis," Bernie said, extending her paw. Jarvis extended his, too, and Mac shook them both. She noticed that Jarvis didn't say anything and asked, "Is he all right?"

"Yeah," said Bernie. "He'll be fine. Just a little . . . uh . . . seasick."

"We haven't even left the dock!" said Mac with a chuckle. "Besides, the *Stargazer* is technically out of commission. We only use her for meetings and communications. We never take her out to sea."

At that, Jarvis's whiskers sprang out of their melancholy droop.

A voice from the kitchen called out, and Mac replied, "Be right there!" As she scurried away, she yelled back over her shoulder, "Bon appetit!"

The promise of the *Stargazer* not going out to sea was like a magical spell that reinvigorated Jarvis. With bright eyes he pushed back his hood and then, as if seeing the bubbling fondue for the first time, took a big, long whiff.

"Bern, could you pass the Tabasco?" he asked happily.

Bernie smiled and handed it to him. It was nice to see him back to his old self. As he sprinkled it liberally into the simmering pot, she couldn't help thinking how enormous Jarvis's fear of water must be. She'd never seen him so sullen and withdrawn!

Meanwhile, the words "we never take her out to sea" had had the opposite effect on Bernie. What was the point of being on such a cool boat if you couldn't take it out into the ocean? Where was the adventure in that? What kind of mission was this? She joined in with Jarvis and dipped a hunk of crusty French bread into the pot, hoping her disappointment would melt away like the savory cheese.

Once Bernie and Jarvis had devoured the fondue, Mac reappeared from the kitchen, wiping her hands on a dish towel.

"How was it?" she asked.

"*So* good!" said Jarvis, dabbing at his whiskers with a napkin. Bernie was about to agree, but something caught her eye. Mac's sleeves were rolled up, and a series of strange scars and marks twisted around her right arm. Mac caught her looking and her cheery expression faded.

"It happened on my last undersea mission," confessed the cook.

"What did?" asked Bernie quietly.

"I don't know if I should tell you. It was too horrible," said Mac, shuddering. She slid the sleeve of her right arm up a little more so Bernie and Jarvis could see the strange patterned scar even more clearly.

"I got stuck in a sea urchin," said Mac darkly. "It took a dozen Mouse Watch divers to get me free. I almost didn't make it." She glanced from the scars back up to Bernie and Jarvis, and then, leaning forward a little, she whispered, "If you have a choice whether to go underwater or not, my advice is simple. Don't. Beg Gadget Hackwrench for a different assignment. It's dangerous down there for a mouse. There are monsters so horrible they'll give you nightmares."

As she turned to go back to the kitchen, Bernie and Jarvis exchanged a long glance. Jarvis looked so unnerved that his furry face had gone the color of chalk.

"You don't think they'll make us go underwater, do you?" he squeaked.

Bernie was about to reply when she heard a ping from her smart watch.

"The meeting's in five minutes," she said quietly. "I guess we'd better go."

Bernie and Jarvis called "Thank you!" to Mac, then hurried out of the mess hall and down the winding corridors, following the signs to the navigation room, where they were supposed to meet Chip and Dale. As she ran, Bernie's heart thudded with excitement—and a little bit of fear. Was there a chance that they'd actually go underwater? She was really going to help the legendary chipmunks on a mission, but she couldn't help wondering just how much danger they might actually be stepping—or diving—into.

CHAPTER 5

"Right on time," said Chip briskly. "Good. We have a lot to cover!"

Bernie and Jarvis sat at an immense conference table. On the walls were various maps and nautical charts, most of them old and out-of-date. Contrasting with the historic surroundings were the brand-new computer monitors lining the walls and the seventy-inch flat screen that was suspended from the ceiling.

"Ooh, check out this old closed-circuit radio!" Jarvis exclaimed, fiddling with the dials on an old-fashioned-looking box in the corner. Suddenly, it started beeping. "Oops."

"Jarvie, what did you do?" said Bernie.

"Don't worry," said Dale, "that old thing has been sitting here for years—there's no way it's still operational."

"Actually," said Chip, "that's why we brought you here.

Gadget wants us to clean and organize the *Stargazer* and take inventory of all this old equipment—"

"And we thought it would be a fun history lesson for our two newest recruits while the rest of the Watch is away," finished Dale. "Now . . ."

But he didn't finish his thought, because a new voice crackled to life through the radio speakers.

"This is Delta Theta Four, this is Delta Theta Four, with a secure transmission. The SS *Moon* has been located. Repeat, the SS *Moon* has been located. Coordinates are thirty-three point nine nine eight zero two eight, minus one hundred nineteen point seven seven two nine four nine. Repeat. . . . Coordinates are . . ."

The voice kept cutting in and out amid static.

Chip's and Dale's jaws practically hit the floor. Bernie and Jarvis exchanged confused glances. What was the SS *Moon*?

"Wait!" cried Chip. "Turn that up!" Jarvis turned up the volume, but it didn't make the transmission any clearer.

"Minus one hundred nineteen . . ." Dale was frantically typing the numbers into one of the computers.

"Did you hear the rest of it, Chip?"

"Ahhh," said Jarvis, panicking. "What did I do? Did I hit the wrong button?"

"This is Delta Theta Four, over and out." The static crackled, and then the radio went silent again.

"Nooo!" yelled Chip, diving for the radio and fiddling with the buttons. "We need the rest of the coordinates!"

"Here's what I was able to get," said Dale, showing Chip what he had typed into the computer. "Think we can use this to figure out the rest? Slinktail, you're good at puzzles. . . ."

Bernie's head was spinning. "What's going on?!" she shouted above the chaos.

"Well, I guess plans have changed," said Chip, turning to Bernie and Jarvis.

"What plans? What's changed?" asked Bernie. But despite the chaos, she was excited. She had a feeling something big was happening that was way more fun than organizing the Stargazer.

"It seems," said Dale, "that we just intercepted a very important transmission. The SS Moon has been found."

"At least, it was when that transmission was first sent," added Chip. "It's new to us, but who knows when it was first sent. It could have been floating around out there for years."

"What's the SS Moon?" asked Bernie.

"It's a long-lost spy submarine from when American mice helped out during the Cold War. Mice have been searching for it for decades, but no one has been able to find it—until now. If this transmission is really true, it could be one of the most important finds in a century!"

Bernie glanced at Jarvis, with excitement dancing in her eyes. Jarvis looked apprehensively back at her, as if he didn't trust or like the direction the conversation was going in. Sunken ships and underwater discoveries didn't bode well for the lanky rat. Especially after hearing Mac's description of underwater monsters that should be avoided at all costs!

"Why is it so important?" Jarvis asked, looking like he didn't really want to know the answer.

Dale typed something into the laptop, and an image of a silver disc filled the screen.

"What's that, a UFO?" asked Bernie.

"It's a saucer, but not a flying one," said Dale with a chuckle.

"It's nicknamed the Milk Saucer. It comes from the name Million Kilowatt Generator, which got abbreviated MIL-K Generator during World War II. Over time, it was simply called MILK or the Milk Saucer by most of the troops because of its shape," said Chip. "Supposedly it's an energy source so powerful that it can destroy an entire planet. Nobody is really sure if it exists or not. Rumors say it was on board the SS *Moon* when the sub disappeared. Some thought it vanished into the Bermuda Triangle. Some say it was destroyed by enemy torpedoes. I say that's nonsense—if it was, none of us would be here. It has long been given up for lost. This transmission changes everything."

"If it is out there," added Dale, "we just have to make sure we get to it first. If it ever fell into the wrong hands . . . well, let's just say this just got bumped up to priority number one."

"We're talking potential worldwide destruction here," said Chip. "If we were able to receive that transmission, I bet R.A.T.S. could, too. That means the race to get to the SS *Moon* first is on."

"So, what . . . um . . . what do you expect us to do?" asked Jarvis nervously. "Is there an underwater drone that we could, like, remotely pilot from here? Something that could dive down to the wreck and get the Milk Saucer before the R.A.T.S. do?" He glanced anxiously at Chip and Dale. "I'm really good at piloting drones!"

"I'm guessing that it's probably too deep for a remotely piloted vehicle," said Chip, shaking his head. "We've got to go in ourselves. But worry not, we're going to contact the best submarine captain in the Mouse Watch fleet."

"Who's that?" asked Bernie.

"Captain Phineas Crumb," said Chip. "He should be able to help us figure out what to do next."

"Meanwhile, I've plugged in the incomplete coordinates," said Dale. Bernie watched as he pressed a few buttons and a map appeared on the computer screen. "It looks like it's in this general region, somewhere off the Mediterranean coast."

Chip circled the area with a digital pen. "We've got to get there quickly. That transmission could already be in the wrong hands. Crumb can help us figure out the exact location once we're down there. In a nutshell, it's vitally important that we find it before the R.A.T.S. do, so—"

"Nutshell?" interrupted Dale. "What nutshell? Is there a peanut involved in this plan? I'm starving."

"Not a real nut— Oh, forget it," Chip said. He turned back to Bernie and Jarvis. "Are you two ready? I know it's a lot to ask for a couple of Level One agents, but you can handle it. You guys really impressed us back in New York, and we know you won't let us down."

"But how likely is it that we can find it? I've heard that some shipwrecks are never found in spite of treasure hunters having expert technology," said Jarvis.

Chip and Dale shared a glance. "Oh, you can be sure that they don't have anything close to the technology Gadget will provide. Even if we don't know where it is exactly, you can bet that we'll get there. It might take some detective work, but you're Mouse Watch agents, right? You've got this!"

Chip pressed a hidden switch beneath the conference

table. From somewhere deep underneath the *Stargazer*, a powerful engine rumbled to life. Bernie felt the floor begin to shudder and vibrate. Then, to her surprise, an entire wall of the navigation room slid slowly to the side, revealing a huge hidden chamber.

There, displayed before them, was a sleek, aerodynamic vessel made of nonreflective black metal. A submarine.

Wow!

If she had to guess, Bernie assumed that the sub was probably half the size of the *Stargazer*. It had been hidden so cleverly inside the old vessel that from the outside, nobody could know this historic relic of a ship housed the most futuristic-looking vehicle Bernie had ever seen.

"This is the SS *Cheese Dip*, and it will be your home for the next week and a half," said Chip.

"Wait," said Jarvis, his fur turning white. "You're not coming with us?"

"We have to stay here and hold down the fort," said Chip. He glanced at his smart watch. "Okay, you'll have exactly forty-eight hours to complete the mission, so start synchronizing your watches now, recruits."

After Bernie and Jarvis did what he'd asked, coordinating their mission countdown times, Bernie was surprised when she looked up and saw a little bit of good-natured jealousy in Chip's expression. "Back when

Dale and I were younger, we would have jumped at this chance, right, Dale?"

Dale nodded eagerly. "Searching for sunken treasure? Sign me up!"

Chip stepped forward and shook Bernie's paw. "Congratulations, you two, you're headed for the bottom of the ocean!"

They were startled by the sound of something heavy hitting the floor.

Jarvis had fainted on the spot.

CHAPTER 6

"Yes, sir. I know, sir. I won't let you down, sir."

Juno Yellowfang hung up her rat-size phone. She felt miserable.

She gathered her tattered, puffy green vest—a cast-off from a 1980s fashion doll—tightly around her as she shuffled through her dingy quarters.

Why did I ever sign up for this? she wondered. *I could have had a nice, cushy life behind a cheese shop in France, but no. I had to go and sign up to join the stupid R.A.T.S.*

She pressed a button and a hidden wall in the fortified R.A.T.S. warehouse swung around in a semicircle. Stepping behind it, she descended a set of rusted iron stairs to a dank cavern below.

"You're supersmart," they said. "There's no place for a rat in the city," they said. "Join the R.A.T.S., help our cause. You'll have job satisfaction!" they said.

"They" were obviously wrong.

She'd been miserable since day one.

"I think I'm coming down with something," Juno muttered to herself. She reached into her pocket for a piece of tissue and blew her nose. She missed Jarvis. He was the only one who had ever been nice to her.

Where was he now?

As she reached the bottom of the long, twirling staircase she thought back to her conversation with the boss.

"I'm going to give you one more chance to impress me, Juno. Operation C.L.A.W. requires two phases. Phase one will be under your direction."

She'd felt confused. "Operation C.L.A.W.? Sir, I don't think you told me about this one."

"Of course I did," he'd said, his voice calm and low. "You need to keep more organized records of our conversations, Juno."

Juno didn't need to take notes. She had an excellent memory, and she'd never heard that operation mentioned even once.

"The Continent-Leveling Apocalypse Weapon. With it I can bend the entire world into submission. It is my most prized invention. But I have yet to find an energy source powerful enough to fuel it—until now. Juno, we must go to the moon."

"The moon, sir?"

"The SS *Moon*. We have just intercepted a *very* interesting transmission. A source of power called the Milk Saucer, long thought lost, has reappeared aboard an old submarine. I have another agent who will be handling its retrieval. But I have a special job for you. Two young Mouse Watch agents made quite a mess of Thornpaw's attempt to take over New York City. I want you to make absolutely sure that they do not thwart my plans this time, too."

"Wh-wh-which agents, sir?" Juno had asked.

"Bernadette Skampersky and Jarvis Slinktail," the boss had said.

Juno's knees had started to shake at that part. If there was one thing that all the rats hated, it was when the boss gave them an important job to do. It was nearly impossible to make him happy no matter how good you were. But Juno's knees had trembled for a different reason this time. Jarvis Slinktail was her friend! At least, he had been. He'd left to join the Mouse Watch and tried to get her to come with him.

I should quit now. I can't do anything bad to Jarvis!

The whole mission left her feeling sick.

Juno opened a locked steel door. The rusty hinges screamed in protest. The room was pitch-black except for a single beam of watery light that illumined a figure in the center. The *thing* that was in there crouched, rather than sat, on a simple wooden stool. The aura she projected was of something sick, something that should have died a long, long time ago but was somehow kept alive by hate itself.

She was more than just a rat.

She was a force of nature.

Juno noticed that the hairs of her chin were straggly and gray, and a bit of green spittle dotted her leathery lips. But Juno also knew that she was exceptional in ways that were important to her boss, ways that could serve his purposes.

The rat's name was Abiatha Squint, and she was one of the most ferocious rat fighters in R.A.T.S. history.

She jumped off the stool and stood before Juno, deferential but scowling.

"Ms. Squint, my boss, uh, *our boss*, has need of you," Juno said.

Abiatha Squint growled. Juno wondered if Squint was going to speak or not. Finally, after a long moment, in a voice that sounded like old, crinkly paper, she rasped, "Show me my next victim."

Juno suppressed a shudder. She would have hated to be a target for this unthinking, unfeeling monster.

She led Squint back up the stairs to a shabby little office, where a photo of Bernadette and Jarvis was pinned to a wall. Abiatha Squint studied it with interest.

"Young ones," she croaked. "Fun for Abiatha."

Juno didn't know how to respond. The little mouse in

the picture looked nice. Whatever she'd done, she didn't deserve a monster like Abiatha Squint to be stalking her. For that matter, neither did Juno's only friend. What would Jarvis think if he knew she was going along with this? But Juno was too terrified to disagree with the boss, so she followed dutifully along with his orders.

Run, Jarvis and Bernadette, run! thought Juno. *You have no idea the danger that you're in.*

CHAPTER 7

"DIVE! DIVE!"

The captain's voice echoed through the cabin as Bernie Skampersky gazed out of the porthole, watching an array of bubbles float by her window as the high-tech submarine began its descent. Never in a million years would she ever have imagined going to the deepest part of the ocean on a top secret mission for the Mouse Watch.

Just a few months earlier she'd been a wide-eyed, eager recruit anxious to prove herself to the most exclusive group of secret-agent mice on the planet. But now, here she was about to embark on one of the most thrilling and potentially dangerous missions that the Watch had ever tried to accomplish.

I only hope we're not too late, thought Bernie.

She checked her watch. The mission countdown read twenty-seven hours and thirty minutes. *How do they expect us to find the wreck in two days?* thought Bernie. *Seems awfully fast for something that's been lost for fifty years.*

Bernie turned from the window and gazed around the interior of the crowded sub. The elite crew of ten mice were engaged in various tasks, monitoring radar and tracking their progress on miniature, glowing computer screens. The interior of the futuristic vessel was bathed in a red glow, caused by the dim overhead lights that cast eerie shadows on the walls and crew as the sub descended deeper and deeper into the briny sea.

Only one agent seemed to be out of place among the courageous Watchers. Jarvis was biting his fingernails and looking worried. Bernie had had to repeatedly wave the little bottle of Tabasco sauce underneath Jarvis's nose to revive him from his dead faint. But she could tell that for him, waking up inside a submarine with the hatches closed was something horrifying.

I wish I knew how to make him feel better, she thought. She wanted to help him see this as an adventure rather than something to dread.

Bernie walked over to him and stood on her tiptoes to rest a paw on his shoulder.

"Jarvie, look at all the tech! This is everything you

like!" Bernie said, hoping it would distract him from how he was feeling. But the look on Jarvis's face told her right away that no amount of tech could bring him out of his shell. "Hey, check out this map of all the different parts of the sub!"

She traced her finger over the front. "Here's the sonar dome. There's the radar antenna on top of that big finlike thing on the top. It's called the sail. Jarvie, this is all tech stuff. Come here and look!"

Jarvis didn't move. He just sat, staring straight ahead with his hood up.

"Try to relax, Jar," Bernie pleaded. "I'm right here and I'm not going anywhere," she said gently. "I'm 'small but mighty,' remember? I'll look out for you."

Using Jarvis's affectionate description for her usually brought a smile to both of their faces, but Jarvis's eyes barely flickered an acknowledgment.

She tried to think of how he must be feeling, to imagine something that could scare her as much. The only thing she could come up with was cats. Maybe doing this mission for him would have felt like her having to face down a giant tabby.

Now that would be truly horrifying!

A deep, resonant voice interrupted the moment.

"Captain Phineas Crumb at your service!" A jolly-looking, whiskery mouse boomed. "You must be the agents

Chip and Dale told us about. Welcome aboard the SS *Cheese Dip*!"

"Thanks, Captain," said Bernie. "Is there anything we can do to help?"

"Let's start with a tour of the sub! We have some pretty amazing things to show you." He glanced at Jarvis, raising a bushy eyebrow at the quivering, nervous rat.

"Uh . . . is he okay?" Captain Crumb asked.

"Who, Jarvis? He's just fine, aren't you?" Bernie said, elbowing her friend gently in the ribs.

Jarvis jumped and looked up at the captain as if seeing him for the first time. He leapt to his feet and said, "Jarvis Slinktail reporting for duty, sir!" Bernie noticed that in his nervous condition, Jarvis nearly poked his eye with his thumb as he offered a brisk salute.

"No need for the extra formalities, son." Captain Crumb chuckled. "Here aboard the *Dip* everyone knows their job and we offer each other the respect due our positions without a lot of brouhaha!"

Bernie couldn't help but like the stocky captain. And Jarvis, even though he still appeared pale, was doing his very best to act the part of a Mouse Watch agent. Bernie admired him for at least trying.

"Follow me, you two," said the captain. "And I'll show you the greatest undersea vessel that mouse-kind has ever produced."

They followed Captain Crumb as he navigated the narrow corridor, leaving the control room with all of its glowing control panels and radar tracking equipment.

"So, you saw the control room. Most of the stuff in there is for basic submarine operations and for making sure we don't crash into stuff! Haw!" he barked.

From the look on Jarvis's face, he didn't appreciate the light humor.

As they climbed over a step, entering through an opening that Captain Crumb had to duck under, Bernie had an idea.

"Hey, Jar," she whispered. "How about a brain teaser?"

"Huh?" Jarvis asked.

"A brain teaser. Something to distract you. It'll make you feel better," Bernie said.

"I don't really feel like—"

"Okay, try this," Bernie interrupted. "The navy has a brand-new submarine that will only operate if there are exactly twenty passengers on the ship. If the first nineteen seats were taken by average-size mice and the last seat was taken by a massive, overweight rat, then how come it sank?"

Jarvis paled. "That's a horrible riddle! Do you have any idea how I'm feeling right now?" he said.

"Still, you're trying to figure it out, right?" Bernie said with a grin.

"Yeah . . . well . . ." Jarvis's expression had already changed from pure terror to something more like calm concentration.

"See, it's working!" said Bernie.

"Shh! I'm thinking . . ." said Jarvis.

Bernie congratulated herself on the idea. She wished she'd thought of it sooner! The best thing for Jarvis in a crisis was to have his brain occupied with something other than the danger at hand.

The captain led them into a room that was completely different from the one they'd just been in. Bernie gazed at an array of beautifully designed green couches. Each of the comfortable-looking seats was made to fit snugly into the curved submarine walls. Next to the sofas' armrests were gleaming walnut tables with outlets for plugging in tablets and laptops. "How do you power the submarine when you're not connected to the shore?" asked Bernie.

"All of the electricity is generated by the crew. Gadget's idea. Pretty brilliant." He gestured down at the floor. "There are receptor plates built into the sub that harness static electricity to charge the batteries. You'll notice that most of the sub is carpeted. Have you ever touched something metal and made a tiny shock?"

Bernie nodded. Crumb grinned. "Well, it works something like that. The rubber soles of our uniform boots make contact with the carpeted plates, generating a positive and negative charge. It's why we're always on the move here on the *Cheese Dip*. All that scampering around keeps the lights on. Literally! HAW!"

Bernie was glad there was electricity to keep the lights on, since the glowing brass table lamps, each adorned with the SS *Cheese Dip* logo, kept the rooms looking homey and functional. She couldn't stop thinking about how clever Gadget was.

"This is the lounge," Crumb said. "Most of the ship's personnel are currently engaged with getting us under way, but later this evening you'll find this is a favorite gathering place for after-duty activities, board games and such."

"Looks nice!" said Bernie.

"Well, if you think it looks nice now . . ." The captain approached a small hidden door near one of the couches and pulled a switch. In one smooth, silent motion, rectangular panels in the walls and ceiling slid back, revealing wide plate glass windows to the dazzling sea all around them.

Lights on the outside of the sub flared on, revealing a magical underwater vista.

Bernie's mouth fell open. It felt like the sub had fallen away and she was right there swimming in the middle of the ocean!

Schools of shining silver fish darted past the windows, and a gigantic, sleepy-looking red octopus crept along the ocean floor, searching for easy prey. Impossibly tall thickets

of seaweed waved grassy fronds in the undulating current, hiding a few nervous crabs that sought out its shadowy protection. A forest of coral in pink, orange, purple, and yellow hues seemed as tall to Bernie as the Manhattan skyscrapers they'd scampered between just a few short months ago.

It was like visiting the best aquarium in the world, and the sight of it was so wonderful, Bernie could hardly find the words to express how amazing it all was.

"Hey, what's that thing?" asked Bernie, pointing at a strange-looking, fleshy fish that had the face of a grumpy old man.

"Ah, that's a blobfish. Don't see many of those." Crumb chuckled.

"It's so weird!" exclaimed Bernie. "Oh, and what's that cute little guy?" She asked about a little yellow ball with tentacles and two floppy fins where its ears should be.

"That? It's a Dumbo octopus."

"I want one!" said Bernie. The cute yellow ball swam right up to the window. Its big fin ears flopped comically, and its tiny tentacles undulated, making it look like it was waving to them.

"Hi there," cooed Bernie. "Jar, you need to come and look at this! You're missing all the good stuff!"

Captain Crumb chuckled at her expression as if he understood exactly what she felt.

"You'll never forget the first time you see the ocean like

this. Really something, eh? And we're not nearly as deep as we're goin' to be. After this shelf drops off, we'll be going to some truly fascinating places in the briny deep."

Bernie smiled. She glanced over to Jarvis but saw, with a mixture of relief and disappointment, that he'd barely noticed the amazing sea life at all. He was slumped on the floor with his brow furrowed beneath his blond bangs, puzzling out the riddle that Bernie had given him and staring into space. He looked like he was a million miles away.

Well, it's better than the alternative, Bernie thought. She glanced out the window and saw a dinosaur-size eel poking its ferocious-looking head out from between a couple of ancient rocks. *But what a shame to miss all this!*

"Your quarters are behind that door," said Captain Crumb, indicating a hatchway at the back of the room. "You'll find your luggage, new uniforms, and some special underwater training equipment sent over from Gadget. Dinner is served in the mess hall at eighteen hundred hours."

"That's six o'clock, right?" asked Bernie.

"You know your military time! Well done," Crumb said.

Bernie grinned. She was glad she'd studied how military time worked back at school in Thousand Acorns. Noon was 1200 hours—that was easy to remember, because it looked like twelve o'clock. Then you just kept adding one hundred every hour. One p.m. was 1300 hours. Two p.m.

was 1400, and so on until midnight, which was 2400 hours. It was easy once she'd gotten the hang of it.

"And make sure you rest up tonight," said Crumb. "You'll be woken up bright and early tomorrow morning for special undersea training, and it'll be intensive. We don't have as much time as I'd like to get you ready for our rescue operation, but we should at least be able to get you the basics before we reach the shipwreck. The rest you'll have to learn on the job."

"We'll give one hundred percent, sir!" said Bernie, offering a quick salute.

"I'm sure *you* will," said the captain. The bushy-whiskered mouse shot a dubious glance over at the distracted Jarvis. "But the question is, will *he*?"

CHAPTER 8

Dinner was a delicious selection of crackers and imported cheese. Bernie was happy to find that Mac, in spite of her reservations about sea monsters, had also come along on the journey. After sampling her delicious fondue back on the *Stargazer*, Bernie knew that even if the mission was scary and dangerous at least they would be able to calm their nerves with tasty, mouth-watering meals.

Jarvis was completely absorbed with trying to solve Bernie's brainteaser and barely tasted his dinner. Bernie wished he would get a little more excited about the mission they were on, but she was happy at least to see him distracted from his fears of imminent death. He asked her question after question as he doused his dinner with Tabasco sauce.

"What's the average weight of each person on board the vessel?" asked Jarvis.

"Irrelevant," replied Bernie, wiping cracker crumbs from her whiskers.

"How was it made?" asked Jarvis. "Was it assembled with old tech, like rivets and stuff? Maybe it sprang a leak and that's why it sank."

"Nope, not even close," said Bernie, taking a big drink of Whiskerfizz, her favorite soda pop. It was popular with the younger Mouse Watch agents. "Keep thinking."

Jarvis grinned. "I like this one. It's tricky!"

Bernie smiled back. She made sure not to bring up anything about the mission in case it would pull him out of his reverie. She wanted to keep him as calm as possible.

After dinner, they found their individual cabins and settled down for the night. The sub didn't have its exterior lights turned on, making it impossible to see the vibrant ocean life outside her porthole windows. But the thought of all the amazing things floating by outside filled her with curiosity and excitement.

Despite the events of the past few days, Bernie was far from tired. She knew she should be worried about the R.A.T.S. Milk Saucer first, and all the potential danger that lurked out there in the dark waters beyond her window, but right then all she wanted to do was enjoy the journey.

She changed into her favorite pajamas. At the foot of her bed was a small locker, which she opened to find a brand-new underwater uniform. It was black and felt a little slippery to the touch but wasn't quite as thick as a wetsuit. It was obviously waterproof and designed for both shipboard and underwater use.

"I'll bet Gadget designed these," she murmured. The black suit was decorated with seafoam-green trim and had the words SS *Cheese Dip* embroidered in gold thread on the front, and her last name, Skampersky, on the back.

Under the uniform was a metal box. Bernie picked it up and was surprised to discover a gleaming white plate on the outside, with the outline of a paw on it.

A haptic sensor lock? Whatever was in the box must have been top secret. She placed her paw on the outline to see if it would do anything, but the plate just glowed red.

No dice.

Bernie put her paws on her hips and stared down at the mysterious box. *Hmm. Maybe only the captain can open this. Rats!*

She crawled into her bunk beneath the porthole and drew the soft woolen blanket up to her chin. The hum of the submarine engines was far below her and it created soothing white noise. At first, she thought she might spend a little time reading a book, but the day had been filled with so much activity that, to her surprise, it wasn't but a few seconds later that her eyes grew heavy and she fell into a very deep, very relaxed sleep.

But it didn't last long.

She'd been having a wonderful dream about sprouting a fish's tail and becoming a mermouse. She was racing a stingray and having a great time when suddenly the loud, shrill sound of a bosun's whistle startled her awake.

"*Up and at 'em!*" roared the captain's voice, echoing through the scuppers, a series of tubes that were positioned throughout the ship for communicating. "*Check your watches, agents! We've got seventeen hours and fifteen minutes to get this mission done. Training begins in ten minutes in the aft salon. Move, move, move!*"

It wasn't her favorite way to wake up, but Bernie wasn't the lazy type. *We're burning daylight!* she thought as she leapt out of her bunk and groggily made her way to the small shower. Then, after quickly dressing and making sure her blue hair was styled into her signature pouf, she grabbed the small metal box at the bottom of her locker and followed the signs to the area the captain had indicated.

When she arrived, she was surprised that Jarvis hadn't gotten there before her. The lanky rat had a thing about punctuality and was almost always early.

Uh-oh, Bernie thought. *I hope he's okay.*

She didn't have to wait long. A wide-eyed, shaking Jarvis

rounded the corner and rushed up to Bernie. "Subs sink!"

Bernie stared back, confused. "What?" Jarvis looked panicky again and was making no sense at all.

"S-submarines always sink. It's the answer to the b-brain teaser," Jarvis stuttered. "The riddle was, 'The navy has a brand-new submarine that will only operate if there are exactly twenty passengers on the ship. If the first nineteen seats were taken by average-size mice and the last seat was taken by a massive, overweight rat, then how come it sank?' It's a trick question because they ALWAYS sink, that's what submarines do!"

The rat stared around at the interior of the sub as if really seeing where he was for the first time in hours. He looked completely panicked.

"A-and we're sunk. We're sinking and we're SUNK!" he shouted.

"Shhh!" hissed Bernie. "Calm down! The captain will be here any minute!"

"I gotta get out. Gotta get out! Can't breathe!" Jarvis exclaimed. Then, with his eyes bulging, he grabbed his throat and started wheezing and rolling around on the floor.

"You're hyperventilating!" said Bernie, patting his back. "You gotta calm down, Jar! You're freaking yourself out!"

"I . . . (wheeze) . . . gotta . . ."

"What's the meaning of all this?!" came a booming voice. Captain Crumb strode into the training salon with all traces of his jovial expression from the night before completely gone. "On your feet, agents! We don't grovel on the floor in the Mouse Watch!"

His words had a galvanizing effect on them both. Jarvis leapt to his feet and saluted, trembling where he stood. Bernie snapped to as well, hands clasped behind her back and her chest puffed out.

Captain Crumb glowered at them both. "I'm a fair mouse. I like my crew to be happy. But I won't tolerate lack of discipline on my ship, is that clear?"

"Yes, sir!" they said in unison. And even though Jarvis's paws were still trembling a little, he was breathing normally, and Bernie was glad to see that some of his Watcher training had kicked back in.

"Better," said the captain. "Now then, have we got a problem, Slinktail?" He eyed Jarvis with suspicion. "What were you doing on the floor?"

Jarvis fidgeted awkwardly. Bernie saw his discomfort and said, "He had a little too much Tabasco last night. Stomachache. Right, Jarvis?"

She elbowed Jarvis hard in the ribs. Jarvis, taking the cue, nodded miserably.

"Well, stow that bilgewater! We can't have our agents unable to perform while on a mission. I want that Tabasco returned to the galley. Is that clear?"

"Y-yes, sir," squeaked Jarvis, looking crestfallen. Bernie

could tell that the thought of losing his precious condiment made him even more miserable than he already was. Captain Crumb nodded and said, "Okay then. Now, I see you both brought the footlockers Gadget had delivered to your quarters. Let's open them."

After Jarvis and Bernie produced the metal boxes, the big captain placed his paw on each of the haptic readers. As Bernie expected, his prints were immediately recognized, and the white panels slid aside, revealing the contents stowed inside.

"These items are of such a sensitive nature that every precaution had to be taken during their transport here," said Captain Crumb. "We couldn't risk them being stolen in an ambush by R.A.T.S. agents. Please try on the equipment now so I can show you the basic operating procedures."

The first thing Bernie found in her footlocker was a pair of booties for her hind paws. The boots were made of a fabric similar to the new jumpsuit she was wearing and she slipped them on, zipping up the sides.

They fit perfectly. But Bernie couldn't see anything particularly unusual about them.

"Frog feet," said the captain. "Very useful for underwater propulsion. Once underwater, kick your ankles together twice, and they'll grow into motorized flippers. The chances are good that you could outswim a great white shark in those things, and the battery could get you to dry land almost as fast as if you were in a speedboat. Very handy. How do they fit?"

"Great," said Bernie. "It doesn't feel like I'm wearing them at all." She could hardly wait until she was in the water so she could try them out!

The next thing in the locker was a short stick with a bronze sphere on the end of it. A tiny switch was on the handle, and Bernie was about to turn it on when the captain barked, "Not yet! It's called a Jellyfisher. Works the same as man o' war tentacles. If you're attacked by a predator, it will send a jolt of electricity through them that'll make their teeth clatter for a week! Great for putting off sharks or any other giant monster that might decide on a mouse snack."

Jarvis turned pale when Crumb mentioned sharks, and Bernie knew that she'd better come up with another riddle and fast. Her mind raced thinking of all the puzzles her dad had told her while growing up. She waited until the captain was checking a text message on his smart watch and then whispered, "Hey, Jar . . ."

"What?" asked Jarvis, sounding miserable.

"Small boats, five guests in each; sail on land but never on water; busy during the daytime, anchored at night. What am I?"

"Bernie, I don't really want to—" he began, but then his sentence drifted off as a faraway look came over his eyes.

Computer engaged, Bernie thought happily. That'll keep him busy for a bit. It was an old riddle and not the best, but hopefully it would help him get through whatever Captain Crumb had in store for them next.

The last thing in the foot locker proved to be the best. Bernie opened a small case to find a brand-new pair of goggles. They were much like the kind that the Watchers wore as general issue, but these had tight rubber suction seals around the edges and were obviously designed for wearing underwater.

She put them on. A screen flickered to life, displaying an enhanced-reality version of the submarine. It allowed her to see straight through the walls of the sub to an ocean teeming with life. Little pop-up balloons appeared next to each creature, noting its name along with interesting facts and details.

One of the ugliest fish she had ever seen swam lazily by. The pop-up balloon said it was an oarfish. To her it looked like a combination of a shark and a sea serpent. It was very long with a small, square head; a jutting jaw; and a giant, sail-like fin protruding from the top of its head. It was undulating so slowly that Bernie half wondered if it was falling asleep.

"Maybe it should be called a *SNORE*-fish." She chuckled.

"Impressive, eh?" boomed the captain. Bernie jumped. She'd been lost in the spectacular view of the sea life.

"Gadget really outdid herself this time. Your Soggies are fully waterproof and they have an updated operating system that covers everything in the ocean."

"Wait. Did you say 'Soggies'?" asked Bernie.

"Sea Optical Goggles. First we nicknamed them 'Sogs' but eventually it became 'Soggies.' Underwater . . . soggy, get it? HAW!" barked Crumb. "Not only should they help us find clues to lead us to the shipwreck, but they will also digitally map the entire thing when we get there, noting every possible hazard and, hopefully, the location of the Milk Saucer."

Crumb snapped his fingers. "Oh, and also, when the Soggies detect water, a breathing filter engages from beneath the lenses, covering your nose and mouth and enabling you to stay comfortably submerged for up to five hours."

Bernie couldn't believe how much detail she was seeing through the glowing green goggles. The Soggies had a screen resolution far more impressive than the standard-issue Watcher goggles.

"Jar, you really need to try yours on," said Bernie. She noticed that he was holding the case in his paws but hadn't touched them. Like before, he was lost in thought, his mind obsessing over the puzzle that Bernie had given him. He was staring absently, barely aware of his surroundings. It might have helped him cope with his stress, but he was nearly useless otherwise.

Bernie grabbed the sleeve of his aqua suit. "Jarvis, you need to pay atten—"

But she didn't finish her sentence because there was a terrific *BOOOM!*, then the horrible, twisting sound of crunching metal. The impact shook the entire submarine and everyone, including Captain Crumb, was knocked to the floor.

"What just happened?" Jarvis screamed.

Bernie twirled around. At first, all she saw through her goggles was darkness. As her eyes adjusted, she began to make out rows of tall, sharp, white stalagmites and stalactites. It looked like they'd floated into a dark cave.

Except the rocks were moving.

The fur on the back of her neck stood on end when she realized that what she was looking at wasn't the inside of a cave at all. It was the inside of a *mouth*. A cavernous mouth filled with towering, razor-sharp teeth. And they were biting down into the side of the submarine!

"A great white shark!" she cried. There was no mistaking the serrated teeth, which were nearly twice the size of the mouse-size submarine. It must have mistaken the SS *Cheese Dip* for a delicious fish!

Captain Crumb rushed to a scupper and shouted through the mouthpiece, *"We're under attack, evasive maneuvers! Code Red, repeat, CODE RED!"*

There was a whine as the engine torqued the submarine

propellers trying to wrestle free of the monster. Bernie and Jarvis were cast about the cabin as the beast shook the sub in its mighty jaws.

CREEAAAK! The straining metal crumpled. Then, to Bernie's horror, the nearest porthole window began to crack and water trickled through the glass.

If they didn't do something quickly, they would be crushed!

Bernie noticed Jarvis clinging to the edge of a side table, whimpering frantically and hyperventilating. She crawled over beside him and clung to his side. Removing the goggles from his white-knuckled paws wasn't easy, but she managed to pull them away and get them over his head.

It was just in time.

With a smash of shattering glass and torn metal, water blasted into the cabin as if from a fire hose.

Bernie felt an iron grip on the back of her neck as she and Jarvis were suddenly hoisted into the air by the mighty Captain Crumb. The big mouse waded through the rising tide, forcing himself through the ferocious spray, and dove into an adjoining cabin with the two young Watchers in each arm.

Bernie was terrified and watched, helplessly, as the Captain punched a keypad. A big metal door slammed shut, sealing them off from the compromised salon and into a safer part of the submarine.

"We don't have much time left," Captain Crumb said. "Make sure your goggles are secure. I'd hoped to give you some underwater training, but it looks as if you're going to have to learn the hard way. Now, whatever you do, don't—"

But Bernie never heard the end of his sentence. With another horrible crunching sound the SS *Cheese Dip* was chomped in half, the shark's mighty jaws cutting through the submarine like a serrated knife through a tin can.

Suddenly, there was nothing standing between Bernie, Jarvis, and the open ocean.

CHAPTER 9

Thankfully, Bernie and Jarvis didn't have to do anything to activate the breathing apparatus on the Soggies—it kicked into gear automatically. One minute, Bernie was breathing the oxygenated air inside the submarine, and the next, a thin membrane had covered her muzzle, allowing her to breathe normally even though she was floating in the ocean.

At this depth, the sea all around her was icy cold, dark, and ominous. But thanks to the miraculous goggles, she could see everything as clear as day.

She almost wished she couldn't.

The submarine floated by her in two pieces, a mess of flotsam and jetsam, and the giant shark was ravenously trying, rather unsuccessfully, to swallow as much of it as it could chew. Captain Crumb was nowhere to be seen, and, Bernie realized with horror, neither was Jarvis!

"Jar!" she shouted, but all that came out of her mouth was a stream of bubbles. Of course, there was no way to call out to him. She was hundreds of feet below the ocean!

Somehow her message must have gotten through, because a familiar voice piped in through her Soggies.

"B-Bernie! Help!"

"Jarvis? Where are you?" Bernie cried, swimming in circles and trying hard to spot her best friend. Then she remembered that Gadget had designed Mouse Watch goggles to operate on voice command.

"Show me Jarvis Slinktail," Bernie shouted.

The screen of the Soggies shimmered for the briefest of moments and then a map appeared before her, with a glowing dot to indicate Jarvis. Bernie's heart raced when she saw how far away he was. Somehow, during the big chomp, she'd been thrown far from the sub, the current from the pressurized cabin blasting her out of harm's way. But Jarvis hadn't been so lucky. The map showed that he was dangerously near a much larger dot—the shark!

"Hang on, I'm coming!" Bernie shouted. In a flash, she remembered to kick her heels together, activating the powerful frog feet. Her boots expanded into long fins that propelled her forward in a fast *whoooosh!*

"Wheee!" Bernie cried through a rush of bubbles.

It would have been fun if she hadn't been feeling so panicked about reaching Jarvis in time. She sliced through the water quicker than the fastest fish, swimming directly toward the location on her map with no thought at all of the danger she was putting herself into. All she could think of at that moment was Jarvis and getting him to safety.

Seeing the shark from behind the protective barrier of the submarine window was one thing. But swimming right up to it with nothing to protect her was entirely another. She spotted Jarvis, clinging desperately to the side of a couch cushion and holding his Jellyfisher out in front of him. The shark was swimming toward him.

Bernie could tell that despite the frog feet, she wouldn't be fast enough to get to Jarvis before the shark. He was still too far. The tiny Jellyfisher weapon he held suddenly seemed silly and inadequate compared to the massive predator. It would probably register as no more than a bee sting.

As Bernie drew closer, she saw something moving in the darkness behind the shark. She stopped short, swimming in place. A shadowy figure emerged from the murky depths.

It was bigger than the shark.

Bernie's heart pounded in fear as the thing wrapped its python-size tentacles around the unsuspecting great white. Now that it was out of the shadows, she could see it was a dusky golden color and its eyes glowed with bright green fury.

Bernie had seen pictures of a sea creature like this before, but she didn't believe they were real.

A KRAKEN!

Memories of Mac's scarred arm flashed into her brain. She heard the cook's voice saying, *If you have a choice whether to go underwater or not, my advice is simple. Don't. There are monsters down there so horrible they'd give you nightmares.*

The kraken was very possibly the only creature in the entire ocean that could scare a great white shark. As it grasped the shark in its tentacles and squeezed, the great fish thrashed and writhed, gnashing its massive teeth in frustrated rage. It managed to bite down hard on the nearest tentacle, but the kraken didn't cry out or release its prey. It seemed to possess some kind of unearthly power, impervious to the razor-sharp bite. The shark flailed with every muscle it possessed, but the more it fought, the tighter the kraken squeezed.

Bernie was nothing if not brave—it was why she had been recruited to the Mouse Watch in the first place. She wasted no time. Now that that shark was otherwise engaged, she rushed to Jarvis, grabbed him by the back of his uniform, and swam away from the fighting monsters as fast as she could.

The going would have been a bit faster if Jarvis had let go of the couch cushion he was clinging to for dear life. But, to be fair, all of her friend's worst nightmares had suddenly come true, so she could hardly blame him for his death grip on the pillow.

Bernie swam toward a big piece of coral and pulled Jarvis into the shadows behind it.

"I've got you, Jarvie," Bernie said. The rat's chest was heaving, and behind his green-lit Soggies Bernie could see tears flowing down his furry cheeks. She hugged him tightly as she stared back at the terrible spectacle taking place. Captain Crumb and the other crew members were still nowhere to be seen in the murky waters. At first, she couldn't quite muster up the courage to ask her Soggies to find them, afraid that they might be inside the belly of the shark. But then, knowing that it was a Watcher's duty to not leave anyone behind, she whispered, "Show me Captain Crumb and the crew."

The screen shimmered for a moment, then flashed its answer:

Captain Crumb and the Crew are offline.

Bernie's heart sank.

The worst had happened.

The mighty kraken released the great white shark and the terrified animal swam away. But just when Bernie was starting to breathe a sigh of relief thinking they were safe, the creature turned its attention to the spot where Bernie and Jarvis were hiding and swam directly toward them.

"AAAAHH!" Bernie and Jarvis screamed.

They didn't have time to activate their frog feet. They didn't have time to do anything at all. The next thing they knew, the kraken had scooped them up in one giant tentacle.

Bernie and Jarvis were screaming so loudly that Bernie almost didn't notice the small, cleverly crafted bolts that lined the surface of the tentacle. But as the Kraken brought them closer to its vicious, gaping maw, her scream died in her throat.

It wasn't a mouth they were moving toward. It was a window.

"Check oxygen levels," she commanded her Soggies, thinking that maybe a shortage of air was causing her to hallucinate. A readout on her screen confirmed that there was plenty of oxygen left and that the filters in her goggles were working properly.

On the other side of the window was a small figure clad in an old-fashioned brass diving helmet and suit. Was it possible that the kraken wasn't a giant sea creature at all, but a ship?

The tentacle released them from its grip and morphed into a wide, metal staircase. It connected to the side of the ship with a loud CLANG. A door opened.

The figure in the window motioned for them to climb the stairs and enter. Bernie and Jarvis shared an

apprehensive look. She had no idea who or what this was, but if it had saved them from the shark, she reasoned it was probably on their side.

At least she hoped so.

Jarvis, meanwhile, just seemed excited to escape the open ocean and be in the safety of a ship again.

The two friends half scampered, half floated up the stairs and through the door into what was supposed to be the kraken's beak. Once they were safely inside a small room, the door closed behind them, and the sound of hydraulic pumps engaged, draining the water.

They were in some kind of an amazing submarine!

The breathing membrane on Bernie's Soggies retracted, and she was finally able to talk to Jarvis.

"Are you okay?" she asked her friend. Jarvis looked pale. His breathing membrane had retracted, too, and his mouth hung open as he looked around him.

"You both need medical attention," said a low female voice. Bernie glanced up and gasped to see the diver had removed her helmet, revealing that she was a mouse! She had tawny fur and striking violet eyes with long eyelashes. Bernie thought that her eyes looked like the color of storm clouds at sea or coral that was hidden deep under the ocean.

"It's okay," said Bernie. "I don't think either of us are hurt."

"Can't be too careful down here," the mouse said.

The mouse walked to the side of the decompression chamber and removed a conch shell phone receiver from the wall.

"Medic needed in decompression chamber three," she said. "On the double, if you please."

Bernie could tell that this mouse was used to giving orders. When she hung up the phone, she turned back to Bernie and Jarvis and extended her paw.

"My name is Captain Octavia Gillywhisk," she said. "Welcome aboard the *Medusa*."

CHAPTER 10

"Who are you? Where am I? What's that? Get it away from me!" Jarvis thrashed around as the medic tried to check his vitals. He stared around wildly with his chest heaving up and down and his eyes wide. Bernie patted his arm.

"It's okay, Jar, I think we can trust this nice . . . uh, lady," Bernie said, glancing at the submarine captain. "You are *nice*, aren't you?"

"Well, that all depends on who's asking," Octavia said with an arched eyebrow. She had shed her diving suit and was now dressed in an old-fashioned sea captain's uniform: a royal-blue jacket with golden trim, brass buttons, and sparkling epaulets on the shoulders.

"Where are Crumb and the others?" asked Jarvis. "Did you rescue them, too?"

"Yes, yes, they're fine. They were grateful for my

services and were quick to say so," she said, glancing pointedly at the mouse and rat, who were still looking at her defiantly.

"Sorry. Thank you, Captain Octavia," said Bernie, getting the point. "We really are grateful. We could have been eaten back there."

Jarvis nodded and mumbled something similar. It seemed to satisfy Octavia, who smoothed down the front of her uniform, picked at imaginary dust flecks, and said, "The *Medusa* is uniquely equipped for almost any situation. Unfortunately, your submarine, while being a fairly decent piece of tech, lacked certain qualities for surviving down here in the depths."

It was hard to argue. The sub had, after all, been chomped in half!

Bernie realized that although the captain of the *Medusa* had introduced herself, she probably had no idea who *they* were.

"I'm . . . I'm Bernie Skampersky, and this is Jarvis Slinktail. We're agents with the Mouse Watch," said Bernie awkwardly.

"Charmed," replied Octavia.

"Bernie," whispered Jarvis. "I don't know if we should be mentioning who we work for like that. It might be against the rules."

Octavia evidently had sharp ears and overheard the

comment. "Oh, don't worry. I'm familiar with your organization. In fact, I used to be a part of it."

"You *did*?" asked Bernie.

Octavia motioned for them to follow and, as she led them away from the decompression chamber, said, "I learned a lot when I worked for Gadget Hackwrench. She was a great teacher, but in my opinion lacked a certain sense of style. You'll notice that every surface of the *Medusa* is covered with mahogany and brass, unlike Mouse Watch HQ, which is all glass, modern furnishings, and sleek white walls. Ugh."

Bernie was so distracted by what Octavia had said that she barely noticed the beautiful fixtures. "Excuse me, but did you say you worked directly for Gadget?"

"I attained Level Six and was under her tutelage in my youth," said Octavia casually. "I specialized in engineering, so we had that in common. But the truth was, I found the Watch to be a bit limiting. I was never much of a team player. I left to pursue my own, independent interests. And, as you can see, it's been very lucrative." She gestured to the rich mahogany walls trimmed with red velvet curtains. The brass portholes gleamed, and small chandeliers even hung overhead. The inside of the massive kraken looked like something straight out of a Jules Verne book. Where the Mouse Watch specialized in sleekly designed tech that looked futuristic, the inside of the *Medusa* looked old-fashioned, as if it was built in the 1880s.

Bernie thought Octavia sounded a bit braggy, but deep down she kind of admired her, too. Bernie had always struggled with teamwork. It was one of the hardest things she'd had to learn while at the Watch. It seemed that Octavia had been well rewarded for going out on her own.

The captain of the *Medusa* led them through more beautifully furnished staterooms and richly carpeted hallways, going on and on about the craftsmanship and quality of each item. Bernie tried to politely ooh and ahh over each thing Octavia pointed out. She was clearly impressed with herself.

"Oh, wait, I must show you this," said Octavia, stopping in front of a row of brass spyglasses displayed on a velvet-lined tabletop. "These are Spiderglasses," she said.

"You mean 'spyglasses,'" said Jarvis.

"No." Octavia chuckled. "Spiderglasses. They're my own invention."

Feeling curious, Bernie picked up the nearest one, a handheld copper telescope with rich leather accents.

"Unlike a regular telescope, which simply magnifies what you're trying to see, the Spiderglass can help you see in eight different ways . . . the same number of eyes a spider possesses. Just tap the side of the scope and you'll see what I mean," said Octavia.

Bernie did as she was told and was amazed at what she saw. The wall of the *Medusa* vanished with the first tap, and an incredible ocean vista, illuminated with hi-def night vision technology, spread out before her. She jumped when she saw a big sea turtle go gliding by.

"Wow," said Jarvis, swept up with the amazing tech. "Very cool!" He pointed the small telescope in every direction, marveling at the view. "But our Soggies can do that, too," he added.

"Yes, but I'm sure it doesn't look nearly as good," said Octavia smugly.

Oh brother, thought Bernie.

Bernie tapped the side of the telescope a second time and the view changed again. She now had an X-ray view of everything around her. When she looked through the lens, Jarvis and Octavia appeared like living, breathing skeletons!

"Okay, now that's super creepy," Jarvis said, pointing his own scope at Bernie.

Bernie tapped it a third time, and the X-ray vision was replaced by a zoom function so powerful Bernie could see tiny sea insects crawling around on a minnow's fin outside the window. She lowered the scope, smiled politely, and handed it back to Octavia.

"Well, I can see how that would come in handy," she said.

"Humph," said Octavia. "Much more than handy. Necessary. And better than Gadget Hackwrench could have designed," she added under her breath.

Bernie bristled at her insult. Why did she hate Gadget so much? She was the greatest, most heroic mouse Bernie had ever met.

She's jealous, Bernie thought.

Octavia took the Spiderglass from Bernie and put it back on the tabletop. "And that's just three of the settings. It's got five more."

Jarvis handed her his scope. "Great tech. Super impressive!" he said.

Jarvie, don't encourage her! Bernie thought. She was really starting to feel annoyed with their rescuer.

"You're right," said Octavia, smiling proudly. "It is fantastic tech and beyond impressive."

Bernie knew that Jarvis's number-one love was new technology. She wondered if he was as bothered by Octavia's arrogance as she was. Glancing over, she thought he looked completely unruffled.

I should try to be less sensitive, Bernie thought. *A good Mouse Watch agent keeps her emotions under control.*

As Captain Octavia led them on a grand tour of the sub, Bernie grew restless. She could only see so many framed paintings and old photos before they started to look the same, and she was tired of Octavia's constant prattling about the exquisite design and craftsmanship of her ship.

She glanced at her watch. Sixteen hours and fifty-five minutes to go on the mission clock. That was hardly enough time! What if the R.A.T.S. had already found out about the SS *Moon* and were heading there right now? Why were they wasting time on a tour of a sub when they were supposed to be saving the world?

She glanced at Jarvis to see if he shared her concern.

He didn't.

In fact, Jarvis seemed a lot calmer inside the kraken than he was inside the SS *Cheese Dip*, and Bernie wondered if it was because it felt less like a cramped vessel and more like a Victorian mansion.

At the end of the tour, they were led into a large stateroom that had a massive, polished walnut conference table inside of it. Paintings of heroes from Greek myths were hanging on the walls, and the chairs around the table were all covered with purple-striped velvet and had gilded edges.

"First things first," said Octavia, taking the seat at the head of the table.

The captain rang a small brass bell with a seahorse handle. Shortly afterward, several mice entered carrying silver trays, and Bernie observed that each of them was wearing an old British naval uniform—a short blue jacket with a striped shirt underneath—a costume that looked as if it was taken straight from the 1800s.

Bernie's mom was a fashion designer and seamstress, mostly spending her time altering doll clothes from the Springtime Nancy collection. Bernie couldn't help but think that she would be freaking out at the quality craftsmanship.

She'd never mention it to Octavia though.

Octavia noticed Bernie's appraising glance and said, "All of the clothing on the ship is made from the finest quality fabrics. I provide services to some very wealthy clients and I dress my crew well."

"What sorts of services do you offer?" asked Bernie suspiciously.

Octavia smirked. "Oh, all kinds of things. Protection. Transport of various . . . er . . . goods."

There was something about the way she said this that made Bernie feel like Octavia probably had a loose interpretation of maritime law.

The crew returned carrying silver trays laden with gourmet treats. Bernie realized it was kind of hard to keep feeling suspicious of someone when they fed you so well. A sweet-cheese-and-strawberry petit four the size of her own head was placed in front of her. The flavor of the fluffy cake danced on her tongue. The steaming tea served in delicate mouse-size china teacups chased away all thoughts of the freezing ocean water. Bernie soon felt so warm and full it took all of her effort to act like a professional Mouse Watch agent and not curl up in a cozy ball and fall asleep.

"I have a good friend, a mouse named Pierre, who lives beneath a famous bakery in Paris," said Octavia offhandedly. "He graciously supplies us with the finest provisions whenever we put out to sea. These petit fours have been served to the queen herself."

Bernie was happy to see that Jarvis seemed back to his normal self and was eating ravenously. How was it that he was suddenly so comfortable?

"It's all very delicious," said Bernie politely. "But we really need to get going—"

"Simple fare, really," interrupted Captain Octavia, not listening and dabbing delicately at her whiskers with a lavender napkin. Bernie noticed that it matched her eyes perfectly.

"Tomorrow morning, we'll dine with your captain and crew. They're very glad you survived the attack."

Bernie perked up at the mention of Crumb and the crew. "Where are they?"

"Each of the *Medusa*'s tentacles contains a separate wing. Your friends are currently in suites T6-A, T6-B, and T6-C."

"Ah, so each wing is labeled by the tentacle number, Tentacle six, suite A for example?" asked Jarvis.

"Precisely," said Octavia. Then, after giving Jarvis an appraising glance, she added, "You're a quick thinker, aren't you?"

Jarvis blushed at the compliment and mumbled, "Well . . ."

"Know anything about computer systems?" asked Octavia.

"Sure I do!" he replied eagerly.

"Jarvis," interrupted Bernie, feeling the need to change the subject. She didn't want to get too chummy with Octavia. "You haven't solved my riddle yet, remember?"

Jarvis glanced at her and said quickly, "Oh, yeah. 'Small boats, five guests in each; sail on land but never on water; busy during the daytime, anchored at night. What am I?' The answer's 'shoes.' Figured that one out a while ago."

Bernie kicked him under the table. Jarvis looked over and gave her a questioning look.

If Octavia noticed the wordless exchange, she didn't mention it. Instead, she continued on, saying, "The *Medusa* runs one of the most advanced networks ever designed. We have a central server and 10G wireless connectivity all over the ship. I wrote all of the software myself—"

Bernie groaned inwardly as she listened to the captain proceed to rattle off all kinds of additional techspeak she didn't understand. She could tell that Jarvis was doing his best to keep a professional distance but was having a difficult time not engaging with his favorite topic of conversation.

We have no time for this!

She glanced again at her watch. Sixteen hours and forty-three minutes. The little mouse on her watch face seemed to be running faster than before, like it was trying to catch up. Or was it just her imagination?

"I also personally designed our own secure internet search engine," continued Octavia. "We prefer to keep to ourselves down here, don't want any internet location tracking," the captain added.

"Uh, Jarvis . . ." started Bernie.

"Interesting," Jarvis said. "I'm curious, exactly which programming code did you use, Python, Java, or something else?"

"Jarvis . . ." said Bernie again.

"Oh, right," said Jarvis, coming to himself. "Um, sorry, Captain, but we're on an urgent mission. How soon do you think we'll be able to, um, you know . . . get going?"

"A whole section of the *Medusa* is designated as a tech center and workshop," said Octavia. "I've retrieved all the pieces of your submarine and I have a crew of engineers repairing the ship right now. With the help of my nano-bots, the SS *Cheese Dip* should be up and running by morning," she said.

"That's . . . that's . . . incredible!" murmured Jarvis.

"Jarvis!" hissed Bernie.

"I can take you on a tour of the workshop later if you'd like," replied Octavia, overhearing the exchange.

"Would I!" said Jarvis happily. He wheeled around to Bernie and said, "I mean, it couldn't hurt, could it?"

Bernie felt a powerful surge of annoyance. "As soon as our own ship is repaired, we have to get going! We don't have time for a tour of the workshop."

She turned to Octavia and said, "We really, really appreciate you rescuing us, but we are on a rescue mission of our own! I'm sure you understand because you were once a Watcher, too."

Octavia's gaze was chilly. "Of course I understand. As I said before, I've rescued your captain and crew, but they need to rest. You've all been through a harrowing ordeal. If you're a little late on your mission, will it really matter? When I was an agent, I never paid that much attention to the time."

"Yes, it would!" exclaimed Bernie. "The fate of the world could depend on it!"

Octavia chuckled. "Oh, my dear, you have a severely inflated opinion of yourself. You and Jarvis are, what, Level One agents? I'm certain they wouldn't have entrusted two young rodents like yourselves with something that vital to the world's security."

Bernie flushed with anger. She was about to interrupt when Jarvis spoke up first.

"Excuse me, ma'am, but Bernie Skampersky is the greatest Level One agent the Watch has ever seen. I've seen her do things in New York City that even some high-level agents would have had a hard time doing. If she had an inflated view of herself, which she doesn't, it would be well deserved."

He said this calmly and matter of-factly. Bernie blushed with embarrassment and felt a surge of gratitude for her friend.

Octavia held up a paw and continued, acting as if she hadn't heard. "I realize that you feel you're in a hurry, but I insist that you and your friends rest. Your submarine must be repaired before you can leave, so you might as well try to relax." Her eyes flashed dangerously. "Or would you rather be tossed back into the ocean?"

Bernie bit her tongue. She wanted to tell this arrogant mouse what she really thought of her, but she was trying to learn from her past impulsive mistakes. Forcing herself to be calm and taking a note from Jarvis, she replied in a very controlled, even voice.

"Um, I don't mean to be *rude*, Captain," said Bernie. "But how do we know that you're trustworthy? We just met you and don't really know whose side you're on."

Octavia gave a full, throaty laugh. It had a musical quality.

"I'm not on any *side* but my own," she said. "The *Medusa* helps the highest bidder if we help anyone at all."

"Um, are you a pirate?" asked Jarvis.

"Arrgh!" replied Octavia, squinting her eyes and grinning. "It be a great way to make a livin', matey."

Jarvis smiled politely at her impression, but Bernie felt doubly annoyed. She believed Octavia was evading her question.

"Okay, well, have you talked with Captain Crumb? Did he make some kind of arrangement or whatever with you?" asked Bernie.

"He did. I've agreed to repair your ship in exchange for a few items I need for the *Medusa*. However, in case you're wondering, I told him that I won't have any part in the shipwreck you're looking for. It's far too dangerous. I advised him to steer clear, but he seems like the stubborn sort."

"He's not stubborn! We're on an important mission, trying to save the world. We're agents of the Mouse Watch. Helping others in need is what we do, free of charge."

She was about to add, *We're not just out for ourselves, like you!* but she just managed to hold her tongue.

"Well, it doesn't seem like a very good business plan, but to each their own," said Octavia dismissively. "Now then, since you and your intelligent friend here are my guests, I suggest you retire to the guest quarters."

At that, she stood up from the table and rang a bell.

A couple of crew members responded immediately, rushing into the dining room.

"Please escort Miss Skampersky and Mr. Slinktail to their cabins. I believe T2-A and B will be fine."

"Aye, aye!" responded the two gruff-looking mice. And the next thing Bernie knew, she was being shown to her new quarters. She was feeling a mixture of emotions.

She's doing all the right things, Bernie thought. *She rescued us, fed us, and even gave us a nice place to stay. She's definitely arrogant. But is that a reason not to trust her?*

Bernie watched the captain walking in front of her, striding along the hallway firmly in command of herself and the magnificent vessel she'd designed.

I guess she has the right to be proud, thought Bernie. *This ship is really amazing, and she built the entire thing without help.*

But what business does the Mouse Watch have working with a pirate? she thought. *Would Gadget approve of this? But also, what choice do we have? After all, Octavia did save us from disaster.*

Her mind wrestled with the dilemma, and a new thought emerged—one that was even more uncomfortable than the thought of Octavia being a pirate.

What if this is all a trap set up by the R.A.T.S.?

CHAPTER 11

The moon was shrouded by a creeping mist that seemed to envelop the entire marina. All the boats were dark and silent except for one, a ramshackle vessel that was lit by the glow of tiny flashlights held in rodent claws. "What . . . what do you want?" said the old captain, a grizzled human who stared down with wide-eyed disbelief at the rats that had taken him hostage using knitting needles, matches, and a can of hair spray.

"Your boat," said Juno simply. She held one of the penlights fixed on the captain's pale, frightened features.

Something about having to give up his ship, as rickety as it was, seemed to strike a chord. His gaze hardened and he looked like he was about to refuse when, quick as lightning, Abiatha Squint leapt forward and bit him hard on the knee.

"OW!" he shouted.

At the signal from Squint, the other dozen rats with Juno advanced with their knitting needles and sharp crochet hooks and pointed them threateningly at his shin-bones. One of the rats, a big gray one named Snaggle, held a can of hair spray the same size as him, and a match, planning to use it as a flamethrower. He chuckled at the captain with an unpleasant, gurgling laugh.

The captain's feeble attempt at courage failed, and he raised his hands in surrender.

"Tell me where you want to go," he said. "Just don't hurt me."

A few minutes later they were under way, following the weak signal of a tracking beacon to the open sea. The boat rocked up and down as it headed into the breakwater, and Juno couldn't help feeling relief that they were finally on their way. Every moment they spent heading to their destination meant that they were that much closer to the whole mission being over.

But the rats' initial optimism didn't last long when the blip they'd been following vanished suddenly.

Oh great, thought Juno. *Now what are we gonna do?*

Juno glanced back at the diving bell that was being towed behind them, a huge metal ball that acted like a sort of minisubmarine and was equipped with basic navigation controls. It was built much better than the stolen boat. It came directly from the R.A.T.S. lab and was tied to the transom like a dinghy. But the fact that the portable radar had failed made her wonder if once they were inside the diving bell it might leak.

Sometimes, the R.A.T.S. tech just wasn't very good.

Juno sighed. She wondered, not for the first time since joining R.A.T.S., if her life could have taken a much better path. Sandwiched between the ferocious Squint, who had a well-earned reputation for a short temper, and a leaky boat, she considered her odds of either getting clobbered or drowning to be pretty high.

Feeling miserable, Juno rummaged around in the duffel bag she'd brought. Then, after withdrawing a small radio transmitter, she pressed the "On" button and gazed at it skeptically. She'd been assured by the boss that it could intercept underwater transmissions, and that it was coded with hydrophone technology capable of picking up transmissions from any submarines up to thirty miles away.

For a long moment, nothing happened. Then the machine started making noises like a radio tuning to different stations. After a few seconds of static and whiny frequency noises, a green light flashed and a voice crackled over the tinny-sounding speaker.

"This is the *Cheese Dip*. We're on course and heading due west at thirty knots, over."

A second later another voice responded, "Read you

loud and clear, *Cheese Dip*. Maintain radio contact until target is acquired, over and out."

Juno's face brightened. *What do you know, it actually worked!* she thought. It was a bright spot in an otherwise hopeless day. It didn't exactly tell her where her target was, but at least she had the right direction.

"Full speed ahead to the west, Captain, if you please," she said. The grizzled sailor didn't dare protest. One look at Squint and the dangerous rat crew was enough. He swung the old boat in the direction Juno had asked for and accelerated.

As the sea breeze ruffled her whiskers, Juno tried to cheer herself up by imagining that her boss would be pleased she'd selected a vessel with such a low profile. It was so old and worn she had felt certain that if any of the Mouse Watch agents had observed it, they'd have never thought in a million years that an organization like R.A.T.S. would be using it for surveillance.

But just as she had the thought, the engine let out a huge backfire, and a belch of black smoke and sparks flew out of the exhaust.

"Whoops!" said the captain, easing off on the throttle. "Too much juice." The rats growled, but the frightened captain shrugged helplessly. "I c-can get you there, but it won't be fast."

Juno realized that she was completely wrong. She should have grabbed something more reliable, something luxurious like a yacht that had built-in radar, and she felt certain that her decision-making was going to end up being just one more thing her boss would punish her for.

Squint seemed to notice Juno's worry. In her rough, gravelly voice, she said, "Squint always finds her target."

The old crone tapped the side of her wrinkled nose, as if indicating that she could sniff out wherever the young mice were hiding even without technology. Juno knew that Abiatha Squint was legendary but also didn't think that sniffing was possible underwater.

"I don't see how—" Juno began. She stopped short when she noticed Abiatha Squint reach into the pocket of her ratty clothes and remove a small metal object that kind of resembled a fishing lure.

"Got me this from Crispin Jones. He was the worst of 'em, Crispin. Double-crossed Abiatha. But she got this, she did."

Juno had no idea who Crispin Jones was or what kind of a gadget Squint had. But, after Squint twisted the lure, it began emitting a light beeping noise. She looked up at Juno with a watery, yellow eye.

"Say the names of the young agents into this here microphone," she said, pointing at a tiny spot on the lure. Juno, seeing no reason why she shouldn't go along with it, shrugged and said, "Bernadette Skampersky and Jarvis Slinktail."

A tiny light turned from red to green. Squint cackled. "Tracker works by sound. Anytime those two names are said anywhere under the ocean, it'll find the speaker."

Squint dropped it in the water. The lure squiggled off under the waves just like a fish.

As she watched the tracking lure go deep under the water, Juno secretly regretted again having to take part in a mission that put Jarvis Slinktail, the only other kind-hearted rat she'd ever met, in danger. She and Jarvis had history. They'd been friends. They'd secretly played tabletop role-playing games like Mice and Dice together (something that Kryptos would never have approved of).

Jarvis had been so nice to her.

And now she envied the fact that he'd been able to leave and hoped he could, somehow, survive all this.

She wished she had the kind of courage Jarvis had shown, proving that he had enough guts to stand up to the boss and follow a path to a better life.

What if, after this, I left, too? she thought.

She shuddered. The thought gave her goose bumps because it was both exciting and terrifying.

But then a voice in the back of her mind, one that she always tried to ignore, said:

Are you forgetting that you're a rat? Nobody likes rats.

Humans hate us. Exterminators consider us vermin. You'll never be anything but a scrambling trash eater. You're not a hero. You're nothing, Juno.

Nothing.

Juno felt her heart break anew, just like it did a thousand times a day whenever she tried to imagine a better life for herself. She'd been told by everyone, including her parents, that a rat could never afford to dream. And as she surveyed the dismal situation she was in, her misery was complete.

Never dream, she reminded herself.

It hurts too much.

CHAPTER 12

The following morning, Bernie woke up and stared around at the beautiful Victorian-style quarters she was in, complete with a beautiful and super comfy four-poster curtained bed, vanity mirror, and lounging sofa.

Ugh, she thought. *I wonder how Octavia got all this stuff? Somehow, I bet it was illegal—or at least unethical.*

And that unpleasant thought was then followed by another. She realized, for the first time, that all of her luggage and Mouse Watch gear had been inside the SS *Cheese Dip* when it had been destroyed by the shark.

Oh no! she thought. *All my stuff is probably at the bottom of the sea and ruined.* The thought of her land goggles and her uniform, items she'd received after being accepted as a Level One Watcher, meant the world to her. The only other item equally as important was her smart watch.

Thinking about it, she glanced down at her wrist.

Ten hours left!

The familiar cartoon icon version of herself was still running, and the clock was still ticking away the seconds. Anxiety flooded her. Only ten hours! The time was going by so quickly!

She noticed that her aqua suit had been laundered and neatly folded. It had been placed at the foot of her bed on a wooden box. Looking closer, she saw that the big trunk looked just like a pirate's treasure chest.

I wonder what she's got inside of it? she thought.

After lifting the latch and peeking inside, she was disappointed to find that instead of gold doubloons, the chest was filled with various scented bath soaps, shower gels, expensive perfumes, and fluffy bath towels.

"Figures," Bernie groused. However, in spite of her dislike of the submarine captain, she couldn't resist helping herself to a rose-scented bath soap and some lilac fur gel.

After a quick but luxurious shower in a clawfoot bathtub, Bernie was having a very hard time hating Octavia as much as she wanted to. She didn't trust her, but she also had to grudgingly admire her ingenuity and her sense of style.

Still, she's nothing compared to Gadget, she reminded herself. Thinking about her hero brought her a little bit of comfort. Even though Octavia was obviously an amazing engineer, she was out for nobody but herself.

Gadget cared about helping others and that, in Bernie's mind, made all the difference.

After getting dressed, Bernie went to the cabin next to hers and pounded on the door. It took several attempts, but eventually she was rewarded with a groggy Jarvis appearing at the door.

"Hey, Bern. What time is it?" he asked sleepily.

"It's after ten o'clock," Bernie said, holding up her watch so that he could see. "We really need to find Crumb and see if the repairs are done on the *Cheese Dip*. We've only got ten hours left!"

"Wow, is it ten already?" Jarvis said with a big yawn. "I must have really conked out. Here, just give me a quick sec."

Jarvis dashed back into his room to get ready. Bernie couldn't help peeking in after him, and noticed that his room was quite different from her own. Instead of all the frilly Victorian furnishings, Jarvis's room looked like a Victorian tech center.

There were machines that buzzed, spun, sparked, and sizzled. Test tubes bubbled. Large tanks glowed with strange species of sea life. But not everything looked like it belonged in an H. G. Wells novel: On Jarvis's desk, a modern laptop was hooked up to a massive sound system.

It's all he could possibly want, thought Bernie. *Octavia seems to be doing everything in her power to get Jarvis to trust her.*

"Okay, ready!" said Jarvis, bounding out of the bedroom wearing his clean aqua suit. "Let's go!"

"Wait," said Bernie. "After all your fears of drowning and everything that's happened in the last few days, how are you so cheerful?"

Jarvis thought a moment. "I don't really know," he said with a shrug. "Somehow, this ship feels safer to me. Also, even though she's a little 'much,' I have to admit that Captain Octavia really knows her programming. Not that Gadget doesn't, of course," he ended quickly. He knew how defensive Bernie was about her hero. "But it seems like she's been at this a long time and, well, the *Cheese Dip* seems a little sketchy," he added with a shrug.

"Sketchy? Seriously? Come on, Jarvis. You know that Gadget only builds the most advanced tech," Bernie shot back.

"Well, all I know is that only one of two submarines came out of that battle with the shark still intact," said Jarvis. "But, hey, I'm not trying to take sides. You know I'm totally loyal to Gadget and the Watch."

Bernie didn't want to argue with her best friend, so she followed Jarvis out of the room. The fact that he had a point about the shark attack didn't make her feel any better.

We just need to get back to the Cheese Dip *and finish the mission on time. Once we find the Milk Saucer, we won't have to deal with Captain Octavia anymore. Maybe we'll even get promoted to Level Two!*

The optimistic thought helped lift her spirits . . . so much so that she challenged Jarvis to a race to see who could get to the workshop first, even though she didn't know exactly where it was.

When they arrived, both Jarvis and Bernie were huffing, puffing, and even laughing together. Although it was only a couple of days ago, it felt like forever since she and Jarvis had had a chance to goof around.

Just sharing a laugh with her best friend felt great.

"Ahoy, agents Skampersky and Slinktail!" boomed a familiar voice. Both of them looked up to see Captain Crumb's cheery face. Behind him, Bernie saw a newly repaired SS *Cheese Dip* looking almost as good as new. The only noticeable difference was the familiar copper rivets—the same ones Bernie remembered from the kraken—used to close up the seam where the two halves of the sub had been fastened back together.

"Captain Octavia has quite a facility," said Crumb. He gestured to the soaring ceilings and vast array of tools. "I think Gadget would give her favorite wrench for a chance to spend five minutes in here."

"I don't know about that," Bernie mumbled to herself.

Jarvis nodded enthusiastically at the captain. "Did you

know she wrote all the software that powers this ship? She's completely off the grid!"

Captain Crumb raised his bushy eyebrows. "Well, well, look who's come back to life! How come I didn't see this side of you before, Slinktail?"

Jarvis shrugged and shuffled his feet. "Sorry, sir," he said. "I'm not so good in small spaces, I guess. Plus, as evidenced by the stress put on the porthole windows during the shark attack, I think that the engineering on the *Cheese Dip* could have used a little updating."

"Agreed!" came a familiar voice. Bernie saw Captain Octavia stride into the room, this time arrayed in a uniform of soft lilac with embroidered silver nautilus shells on the sleeves. "That's why I've equipped the *Cheese Dip* with titanium-reinforced spars and unbreakable glass. The next shark that tries to make a meal out of that sub will break all its teeth."

Octavia shook hands with Crumb. "We can't thank you enough," said the burly mouse. "The *Cheese Dip* hasn't been called on for a mission in several years. We really needed the upgrade. Rats, like mice, aren't sea creatures, so most of our missions tend to take place topside." Crumb chuckled awkwardly. "It's extremely rare for anything undersea to require our attention, and that's why this mission is so unusual. Unfortunately, that's why making repairs was at the bottom of the list."

"Gadget always underestimated the power of the sea," said Octavia. "Which is why I made it my special project."

Crumb nodded, looking a bit uncomfortable. "Well, ahem, as per our agreement, a shipment of platinum conductors has been approved by Mouse Watch command. You should receive them by the end of day as well as the payment you requested."

"Pleasure doing business with you," said Octavia with a little bow.

Bernie still felt a pang of unease about Octavia. There was something too good to be true about her willingness to help. What if she was secretly working for the R.A.T.S. and had intentionally sabotaged the submarine?

She decided not to bring it up in front of Jarvis. They would probably be back aboard soon, and if he thought the sub was compromised, he'd be useless in the mission to find the Milk Saucer.

"Excuse me, Captain Octavia," said Bernie.

"Yes?"

"During your retrieval, did you happen to find any of my personal belongings? I was kind of hoping that somehow my luggage survived," said Bernie.

The captain shook her head. "I'm sorry. We looked everywhere, combed the entire sea bottom where the accident occurred," she said. Then, turning to Captain Crumb, she added, "The good news is that we found all of your other crew members' personal items. They're on board the sub."

"Much obliged, ma'am," said Crumb. "I'm sure you did the best you could."

"Wait. You're telling me that you found everyone else's stuff but MINE?" said Bernie.

Octavia gazed down and offered Bernie an expression of sympathy that Bernie couldn't help feeling was fake. Then, to add insult to injury, she had the audacity to pat Bernie on the head before leading Captain Crumb and Jarvis away for a tour of the newly repaired sub.

Bernie was outraged! *Nobody, NOBODY, touches my hair without permission!*

And then, the way Octavia pivoted away from the question made Bernie feel both angry and suspicious. *She found everyone else's lost luggage. Somehow, mine has been overlooked. Right. Like that's an accident.* Her tail stuck out straight as a knitting needle, a sure sign she was upset.

I'll bet she's up to something.

But there was no way Bernie could prove it, at least not right then. Feeling frustrated, she tagged along with Crumb and Jarvis and listened to Octavia boast about all the enhancements she'd provided. Worse still, Bernie noticed that Jarvis was glued to the conversation, fascinated by every area that Octavia claimed to have "improved."

When they finished, Captain Crumb doffed his hat. "I

only wish we could convince you to come with us. If you could help us locate the SS *Moon* I'm sure we could make it worth your while."

"I'm sorry, dear Captain, but there's no chance of that at all," said Octavia, her voice growing cold. "If what you've told me is correct and if the Milk Saucer truly is there, then one wrong move and it could blast all the water out of the ocean! My advice to you, like I told your young agents, is to steer clear. Leave it alone. It's not meant to be found."

Captain Crumb hesitated a moment and then, after struggling with some inner decision, he lowered his voice and said, "I wish we could. We have reason to believe that R.A.T.S. may have intercepted the same transmission. If they get to it before we do, we have no doubt they'll use it for nefarious and violent ends. The entire fate of mouse-kind is at stake, not to mention human civilization. We just can't allow that to happen!"

Captain Octavia considered what Crumb had said for a long moment. When she finally spoke, she said a single word.

"Catlantis."

"Did you say 'Catlantis'?" asked the three others in unison.

Octavia nodded. "The lost civilization of cats. They've been living underwater in their own utopian society for thousands of years."

For the first time in the entire mission, Bernie felt her insides turn to jelly. Her paws shook. An underwater city of cats? It sounded like something out of a horror movie!

"B-but I thought cats hated water," said Bernie.

Octavia smirked. "They do. But they are an ancient culture, some say descended from the Egyptian pharaohs' cats. The legends say that because the cats were afraid of water, the gods insisted that they face their fears and sent them to the bottom of the ocean," she said with a shrug. "Who knows if it's true or not. I've only been to their spectacular city once in my travels. But they know everything that is going on under the sea, and if anyone knows the precise location of your shipwreck, it's them."

Bernie's heart was pounding so hard that she felt sure the others in the room could hear it. She'd never heard a concept that had frightened her more in her entire life.

"Your sub is ready, so you can get under way within the hour. The road to Catlantis is dangerous, and I'll escort you," Octavia said. Then, with a meaningful glance at the captain, she added, "And I'll be requiring an extra payment."

"I'm sure we can arrange what you need," said Crumb. "And thank you," he added with a small bow.

"No thanks are necessary," said Octavia, waving him off. "It's business. And I always protect my own interests."

And what exactly are her interests? Bernie wondered.

Bernie and Jarvis exchanged glances. But this time, Bernie felt a lot more scared than Jarvis looked. She remembered how unfazed he was by the kitten rescue, and how he didn't seem to be scared of cats, not like Bernie was. Maybe rats had a different relationship with cats than mice did. Their roles were totally flipped. She felt a terror that only grew bigger and bigger as she imagined what lay in store for them.

An island of cats deep under the sea is absolutely the worst thing I've never thought of.

And then, a newer and more terrifying thought occurred to her.

I wonder how long it has been since they've eaten a mouse?

CHAPTER 13

The send-off feast that Octavia had prepared for them was sumptuous. There were sweet honey cakes with almond butter. Delicate cheese soufflés as light and fluffy as clouds. A seaweed salad gathered from the Sea of Japan with wasabi-seasoned croutons and, best of all, another full-size human pastry for dessert. This one was called a Napoleon and, in any other circumstances, Bernie would have found it to be the second-most delicious thing she'd ever eaten.

But as she sat at the elegant, candlelit table she found that her appetite was totally gone. She couldn't eat when her stomach was doing cartwheels.

Cats. Why, of all things, did the place that they needed most have to be populated with cats? Since she was a tiny mouseling, visions of glowing yellow eyes and slinking felines had haunted her nightmares. Even on the last mission to rescue a kitten, she'd had to do everything in her power to control her fear of being eaten. And that was just ONE kitten! She was about to be surrounded by an entire *city* of cats!

She glanced at Jarvis. He was eating, but not with his usual ravenous abandon. Bernie could tell that he wasn't too happy about the next phase of the mission either. But it had nothing to do with cats—he was scared of getting back aboard the SS *Cheese Dip.*

For the very first time in her life, Bernie found herself doubting the wisdom of having joined the Mouse Watch. She was okay with the death-defying acts of heroism— scaling buildings, flying in drones, sliding down zip lines, and diving deep under the ocean. But the thought of being on an island under the sea with thousands of hungry cats and a submarine that had recently been chomped in half was just too much.

Maybe I should ask Octavia if she can take me home.

She knew what Gadget and the rest of the Watch would say about quitting. They would tell her that when the going gets tough, to work with her team—they needed her, and she needed them. She recited the Mouse Watch motto to herself:

Every part of the Watch is important, from the smallest gear on up. For without each part working together, keeping time is impossible. We never sleep. We never fail. We are there for all who call upon us in their time of need. We are the MOUSE WATCH!

That may have been true, but Octavia seemed to be doing pretty well for herself on her own. *Maybe playing by your own rules isn't such a bad thing,* Bernie thought.

Still, deep down, she couldn't stand the idea of giving up. She'd fought too hard and gone through too much.

Being a Mouse Watch agent was her dream. And her tenacity was what caught Gadget's eye in the first place.

She was going to have to face her fear.

Bernie forced herself to nibble a little bit of the honey cake. Being brave was a decision, and, having made it, she felt a tiny infusion of confidence with the knowledge that she hadn't given herself totally over to the power of fear.

The feast ended with a toast to good fortune, and then, without much of a good-bye, Bernie found herself being ushered back aboard the SS *Cheese Dip* while a stoic-looking Captain Octavia stood at the end of the gangplank.

The regal mouse, standing there with one perfectly manicured eyebrow raised, was the last thing she saw as they closed the hatch. When the lid was secured into place, Bernie thought to herself, *I'll bet she found my Mouse Watch goggles in the wreckage and is keeping them for herself.*

As Bernie climbed down the ladder into the main cabin, she reached up and stroked the edge of the Soggies that were perched on her forehead, reassuring herself that she hadn't forgotten them.

They were her only pair of goggles now and would have to do for all of her future missions.

Bernie's mood improved slightly as the *Cheese Dip* descended once more, and she realized Octavia's improvements on the sub seemed to be as good as she'd said they would be. The new seam around the center of the ship, where the shark had ripped it apart, was airtight.

Well, at least she didn't lie about that, thought Bernie, grateful that leaking was now at the bottom of the list of things to worry about.

Jarvis handled himself better than he had before, even though it was obvious that being aboard the *Cheese Dip* still made him nervous. His faith in Octavia's engineering had obviously made a big impression on him. Although he certainly wasn't happy about being back on a tiny sub at the bottom of the sea, he was able to help out and busied himself with shipboard tasks in order to keep his mind off it.

In fact, everything proceeded fairly smoothly for the first hour or two, with Bernie and Jarvis each managing to keep themselves together emotionally. If Bernie thought about Catlantis too much, she felt waves of panic, so she tried busying herself with every brainteaser she could remember, seeing how many she knew.

But it was impossible to concentrate because she kept

obsessively glancing at her watch. *Eight hours and twelve minutes to go.*

Meanwhile, the SS *Cheese Dip* followed the *Medusa* through the deepest parts of the Pacific Ocean, sometimes catching an extra burst of speed when drifting behind a school of small fish. Crumb's crew was on constant lookout for sharks even though Octavia claimed the ship was more predator-proof than before. Nobody wanted to take any chances on finding out how solid the new construction was unless they had to.

But twenty minutes later, when things suddenly took a turn for the worse, they had a chance to find out.

Bernie had been practicing sailor's knots, a very useful bit of knowledge that could be used undersea or aboveground, when a Klaxon alarm rang through the ship, sending chills up and down her furry back.

"Predator off the port bow!" shouted a voice through the ship's scuppers.

"Evasive maneuvers!" cried Captain Crumb in reply. "All hands to their stations, MOVE!"

Bernie dropped the bowline knot she'd been working on and hurried to the main cockpit. Furry sailors were rushing everywhere, some scanning the radar while others were loading up the ship's torpedo bays. The last time they'd been attacked, they'd had no chance to retaliate.

This time, if Octavia's predictions were true, any creature who tried to bite them would get a solid toothache!

Outside the darkened windows there was a bright electric flash. If they'd been on land, Bernie would have sworn she was looking into a lightning storm.

"What was that?" she shouted.

Captain Crumb turned to face her with a grim expression. "An electric eel. Nasty creature."

"What can we do?" asked Jarvis nervously. "Can we hit it with a torpedo?"

"We're sure as Havarti gonna try," swore the captain. "And we've got something better than a torpedo. We've got just the lightning rod for that electric fish. Ready the Grounder, Agent Fingertwitch!"

The skinny, bespectacled sailor mouse had his paw poised over the Launch button. "Standing by, sir!"

"Fire at will," barked the captain.

"Aye, aye!" said Fingertwitch. Bernie watched as he pressed the button. Outside the ship there was a tremendous WHOOSH. A spray of bubbles shot by the windows as the Grounder—a strange, tube-shaped projectile—shot away from the submarine like a swift underwater arrow.

A screen descended from the ceiling, showing the view outside the ship. Bernie gasped. She could see the eel, ferocious-looking and a good deal bigger than the *Cheese*

Dip. If it wanted to, it could wrap itself completely around their little ship. Blue twines of electricity shot up and down its black, snaky body.

The Grounder sped toward the target, and every breath on board was held as they saw the missile rocketing directly at the frightening beast.

As it drew close, it turned abruptly downward and buried itself in the ground. Then a tiny light poking out of the earth began to flash. The eel twisted and writhed, electricity crackling up and down its sinuous sides. The underwater lightning rod was drawing the bolts of electricity toward it, extracting it from the eel! Judging by the eel's reaction, the process looked extremely uncomfortable. So it did what any creature would do in this situation.

It extended its massive jaws and chomped down on the Grounder, which exploded in a burst of blue light.

Shock waves sent the ship hurtling to one side. The entire crew grabbed on to whatever they could to keep from tumbling over.

"What happened?" shouted Crumb.

Fingertwitch studied his sonar screen for a long moment. Then, after a few seconds in which a pin dropping to the floor would have sounded like an iron bar hitting a sidewalk, the first mate shook his head grimly.

"It destroyed the Grounder, sir."

Captain Crumb didn't waste a second. "Get a second one ready!"

But before Fingertwitch could obey the captain's orders, the interior of the sub grew dark. A gigantic, coiling black mass snaked down around the sides of the ship, blocking all the portholes.

"Oh no! It's got us in its grip!" cried Jarvis.

"But . . . it's impossible!" said Fingertwitch. "Electric eels can't stand the Grounder. It should have swum away!"

"Steady, Slinktail!" shouted Crumb. "Keep it together or I'll order you off the bridge. Where's that second Grounder, Mr. Fingertwitch?"

"The eel is blocking the tubes, sir!" said Fingertwitch. "It's like it knew how to thwart our weapons systems! I . . . I can't believe it!"

ZAAAAAAP!

Blue lightning flickered all around the submarine, crackling up and down the walls. Any mice standing too close to any of the electronic equipment were blown backward and sent crashing to the floor, their fur singed and smoking.

The lights in the sub flickered.

Every computer screen and tablet suddenly winked out.

An eerie silence filled the submarine. Gone was the low, constant hum of engines and machinery that Bernie had grown used to aboard the *Cheese Dip*. That could only mean one thing.

The engines are offline and the backup generator has shorted out!

Panic filled the command center, which had plunged into absolute darkness. Mice were shouting as they tried everything they could do to bring the engines back. Some even shuffled their paws to try to generate static electricity in hopes of reviving the vessel.

But it didn't work. There was nothing that could be done.

Bernie felt the submarine lurch and suddenly come free of the eel's grip.

No wonder mice never go this far below the surface!

But as the *Cheese Dip* continued to drift down, down, down into the darkness, Bernie couldn't resist a single troubling thought:

Why didn't Octavia come to the rescue?

CHAPTER 14

Unbeknownst to both the Mouse Watch and R.A.T.S. as the SS *Cheese Dip* drifted into the terrible blackness, a tiny object secretly attached itself to the immobilized vessel. Abiatha Squint's tracking lure had finally caught up to its target.

On the ocean surface, Juno peered down into the dark water with a worried expression.

The part of her that wanted to do a good job, to please her boss, hoped the tracking device would find the Mouse Watch agents.

But a small voice in the back of her mind hoped very much that her mission would fail.

"Treasonous thoughts," said Abiatha Squint. She tapped the side of her hairy skull. "You doesn't want to do the mission. Can see the conflict in yer peepers. I've seen mutineers before. . . . Dealt with them the way they needed to be dealt with. Cracked bones, I did. Cracked 'em good."

Juno shuddered. Had she been that obvious about her feelings? Did her hatred of her job show on her face? How did Abiatha Squint know?

Juno fiddled with the remote control that she'd used to make the electric eel attack. It was an impressive piece of technology, one that the R.A.T.S. could never have developed if it weren't for the mind-controlling chemicals in the cheese spray Dr. Thornpaw had discovered. Finding the eel and injecting it with chemicals had been a fairly simple task. In fact, Juno thought that overall she'd been doing an adequate job of hiding her feelings and getting the mission done. But evidently, she hadn't done very well. Her loathing for what she was doing was plain as the whiskers on her face.

She turned away, feeling both scared and weirded out by the tough old crone.

Changing the subject, Juno asked, "How will we know when the lure finds the location of the targets? They managed to dispatch our eel. What if it doesn't work?"

Squint spit on the deck of the ship and then replied, "Tracker always works." Then, to confirm what the old rat had just said, Warttoe, a particularly ugly hench rat, pointed at the radar.

"We've picked up the lure's signal. We believe the eel immobilized the sub before it went offline. It's only about five miles to the west of here."

Juno and the rats who weren't guarding the boat's human owner all rushed to see a new green dot on the radar positioned nearby.

"Bring her about and go full speed toward that dot," commanded Juno.

One of the rats guarding the human prodded the captain in the back of the knee with a sharpened crochet hook. The grizzled skipper yelped and shoved the throttle forward.

As the rickety boat resumed the chase, Juno decided that she knew something for certain. Whatever happened, she would not allow herself under any circumstances to be dragged back to the big boss or killed by Squint.

Anything was better than that. If she had to die, then she wanted to choose the method. She didn't want to be tortured. She didn't want to be stomped.

It wouldn't be long now. Soon, in spite of all her misgivings, they would have Bernie Skampersky and Jarvis Slinktail firmly within the R.A.T.S.'s claws.

CHAPTER 15

The interior of the *Cheese Dip* was dark and quiet, lit only by the weak, green glow emanating from the crew's Soggies.

"Jarvis, are you okay?" asked Bernie.

The rat was sitting in front of a laptop, hitting the power button frantically. "Come on!" he murmured. "Come on, come on, COME ON!"

"The batteries are dead, Jarvie," said Bernie. "We used them up hours ago. Besides, we don't have Wi-Fi either, so what's the point?"

"The point? The POINT?" shouted Jarvis. "The point is that none of my devices are working! These goggles are nothing more than a night-light without an internet connection! I . . . I've never been this long without being able to access the internet. Look at my paws . . . I'm shaking!"

Bernie watched, feeling bad for her friend.

"I'm sure we'll get the power back on soon," she said, reaching up to pat his shoulder.

"Well, I . . . I'm not . . ." gasped Jarvis. "This is bad. Need hot spot. Somebody, anybody got a personal hot spot? I . . . I've got . . . I need VPN . . . PLEASE!" he cried.

"Jarvie, calm down," Bernie said soothingly. "Seriously, we can figure this out."

Jarvis slumped. He looked down at her with wild, unfocused eyes and said shakily, "Okay, okay . . . I'll be okay."

Bernie rolled her eyes. "Besides, it's just technology."

Jarvis steadied his breathing. "Wh- . . . what do you mean?"

"We're on a mission, Jar. We can't afford any distractions. Time is ticking down!"

"Wait. What?" said Jarvis, suddenly focused. "You think I don't know that? I care about the mission, okay? But I also need certain things to feel . . . safe, okay? And technology makes me feel safe! Even Octavia understands that!"

Bernie turned away from him and stared out the window. Because the goggles weren't connected to the submarine's Wi-Fi she couldn't see anything outside and everything looked murky and dark.

"Forget it," said Bernie flatly.

Jarvis hesitantly approached. "I don't get it. What did I do? I . . . I love technology. I *need* technology. But why are you mad?"

Bernie wheeled on him. "I don't want to hear about Octavia, okay? I think she's arrogant, suspicious, and sneaky!"

"Sneaky? How?" said Jarvis. He was so thoroughly confused by the direction the conversation was going that all signs of his internet addiction were temporarily forgotten.

"Just . . . sneaky!" said Bernie. "And nobody sees it but me!"

"She's not that bad," said Jarvis. "She's a little arrogant, but she totally helped us."

Bernie crossed her arms. "Oh really? Where was she when the eel attacked, huh?"

Jarvis stared at her for a moment with his mouth slightly open. Then he brushed her comment aside with a wave of his paw. "She . . . she was probably gathering some resources or something and didn't see it happen."

"Yeah, like I believe that," said Bernie.

"Attention, crew!" came Crumb's voice through the scuppers. "All hands to the bridge."

Bernie brushed past a confused Jarvis. "Come on, we'd better go," she said.

In the control center, Captain Crumb had a chart unrolled on a navigation table and was studying it intently. Like the others, he had his Soggies on and had to squint through the lenses to make out the colored lines on the map.

"Skampersky, Slinktail, looks like you're going swimming," said Crumb.

"S- . . . swim- . . . swimming?" stuttered Jarvis.

"Swimming," said Crumb. "Underwater diving, to be precise. We can't afford to send any crew members, and since you two are brave agents of the Mouse Watch, this should be right up your alley."

He pointed a thick forefinger at a spot on the map. "About six months ago a human oil tanker went down not one hundred yards from where we are. The plan is to go and recharge our primary power source. Fingertwitch!"

The skinny, bespectacled mouse dashed up holding a titanium cylinder. Bernie was surprised to see that it was so tiny.

"That?" She pointed at the titanium tube. "That's what powers the entire submarine?"

Crumb nodded. "Another of Gadget's inventions. It will stay charged for months if it comes in contact with a battery. The bad thing is, if it is *overcharged*, it goes completely dead. A trickle of static electricity is too weak to bring it back to life."

"So, the electric eel was what shorted it out?" asked Bernie.

"Exactly," said Crumb. "Now, all you have to do is get this within six inches of a powerful, active battery like the one on that ship and it will charge. Your job will be to pop over to the wreck, charge this baby, and swim back. Shouldn't take more than ten minutes with your frog feet."

Bernie was glad for the diversion, something to get her mind off of both Catlantis and her frustration with Jarvis. Jarvis, of course, hated the whole idea.

Bernie glanced at him. His expression was blank. His jaw moved soundlessly up and down as if he was desperate to find an excuse but couldn't come up with one.

The next thing they knew, both mice were in the decompression chamber of the sub and were being given last-minute instructions by Fingertwitch.

"Just breathe normally. Your Soggies might not have internet access, but the oxygen function will work fine, so don't panic," he said, sternly staring at Jarvis. "The ocean current might be a bit tricky," he added. "Before the sub went down, I got a weather report that there might be a monsoon on the way at the surface. Oh, and if all else fails, watch the fish."

"The fish?" asked Bernie.

Fingertwitch nodded. "Watch how they swim and follow them. Their movements. Their instincts. They know what they're doing and how to avoid danger."

Jarvis looked confused, but gulped and nodded. Bernie noticed that he was white as a sheet.

"Good luck," Mr. Fingertwitch said as he closed and sealed the door to the room. The next thing Bernie knew, seawater was filling up the room and a door in the back of the sub had opened, plunging the two of them back into the briny deep.

CHAPTER 16

The Soggies' low power mode allowed for night vision, underwater breathing, and, thankfully, two-way radio communication. Jarvis was especially relieved that they were able to stay in contact as they made their way toward the sunken ship. Bernie noticed he was shaking when he first got back into the water. However, with the help of his frog feet, Jarvis was almost able to keep up with Bernie as long as he kept his arms at his sides and let the motorized flippers do the work.

"Jarvis, you're still behind me, right?" said Bernie over the radio. She was thankful for all the years of swimming lessons that her mom forced her to have in a big green Tupperware bowl when she was little. In spite of the darkness, she found the whole experience of being deep underwater exhilarating.

"I-I'm here," stammered Jarvis.

Bernie recalled the signposts that Fingertwitch had pointed to on the map and was glad to see, after a few more minutes of swimming, the hazy outline of an enormous tanker coming up on their left. They had to navigate past a huge forest of seaweed, but other than a few particularly large hermit crabs, there was nothing dangerous standing between them and the big boat.

As they swam close, Bernie saw an enormous hole in the side of the tanker and wondered what had happened to sink it.

An explosion? she wondered. The inside was dark, and greenish-black algae clung to the ragged sides of the blown-out metal. Bernie clicked her heels together, turning off the frog feet. Jarvis drew up beside her shortly after and hovered awkwardly, trying to float in one place.

"I don't like the look of it in there," said Jarvis. Bernie could hear his rapid breathing and knew that if they didn't keep moving, he'd probably lose his nerve and bolt back to the *Cheese Dip*.

"We don't have to like it. We just have to recharge the battery so we can make it to the Milk Saucer," said Bernie. "Come on, we got this."

She took the battery from a pouch at her belt and swam through the hole.

Inside the tanker, rusted machinery towered over them, and crusty barnacles covered the walls. Crabs and fish roughly the size of Bernie and Jarvis scattered as the green glow of their goggles swept over the crumbling remains.

"Hey, is that the galley?" asked Jarvis.

Bernie turned to where he was looking. A human-size kitchen area with a dining room opened up to her left.

"Looks like it," she said.

"I'm gonna go check it out," said Jarvis, swimming over to a metal pantry. *Of course he would go right for the food.* Bernie was about to tell him to stick with her, but then thought better of it. If Jarvis was preoccupied with foraging for a snack, it might make him less hysterical, which would make it easier for her to do just the job at hand.

"Uh . . . you do that," said Bernie. "Let me know what you find." Since everything was underwater, she had her doubts as to whether he would find anything edible.

Bernie swam along several of the corridors, all of them spookily abandoned. The good news seemed to be that none of the crew had gone down with the ship. She didn't like the idea of running into any human skeletons.

After a few minutes she found the engine room and, with a bit of searching, was able to locate the ship's battery.

Bernie held out her small metal rod, lowering it to within six inches of the ship's bigger battery.

"I sure hope this works," she muttered.

Sure enough, just as she'd been told it would, as soon as the cylinder got close to the power source it began to glow with a faint golden light. She could feel a slight warmth travel up her arm as the *Cheese Dip*'s power source drew energy from the ship's battery.

Then, unexpectedly, her Soggies flickered.

"What? Not now!" she murmured.

Everything went dark. But before Bernie started panicking, the rebooting chime sounded and the Soggies recovered from safe power mode. They must have been drawing power from the newly recharged battery! When the high-tech goggles flicked back on again with all of their functions available, a whole world opened up in front of Bernie's eyes.

The rusted ship was teeming with sea life. Tiny red crabs scuttled over purple and green barnacles. The ship had been magnificent once, and little touches still showed. The engine room still had tools neatly stowed in metal boxes. There was an old record player that, although covered with algae, maintained a sturdy, old-fashioned craftsmanship from the 1950s, and there were old records stacked next to it. The jackets were long since dissolved by the sea, but she could make out part of one label that said "Glenn Miller and His Orchestra." Even though the records were about ten feet from where she stood, the fact that she could read the words on the tattered label proved that the enhanced detail the Soggies provided was stunning.

"Whoa!" she exclaimed. "I forgot how great these things work!" She'd been in low power mode for so long that it was like having had poor eyesight and then suddenly putting on a pair of glasses.

She adjusted the view through the Soggies to cause the ship's walls to appear semi-transparent. She was thankful again that it wasn't like the X-ray vision from Octavia's tech that turned everybody into a skeleton, instead allowing her to understand what she was seeing.

Little tags floated above a school of clown fish, labeling them *Amphiprion ocellaris/percula*.

She saw *Chromis viridis*, the green chromis, a bold-colored fish with glittering greenish scales.

She glanced down at the *Cheese Dip*'s battery, and the goggles displayed a tag that said, SS *Cheese Dip Power Source: Charging*.

"Sweet!"

She repocketed the *Cheese Dip*'s battery in the pouch at her belt and swam back to get Jarvis. The entire operation had gone off without a hitch so far. Now, if they could just get back to the sub without any more problems, she could finally feel like she'd accomplished a task for the Mouse Watch without any curveballs.

But as she got back to the galley, she was surprised to find that Jarvis wasn't there.

"Jar?" she said cautiously. When there was no answer she called again, "Jarvis!"

Everything was eerily still and quiet.

Suddenly, she felt something touching her shoulder!

"AAAHHH!" Bernie wheeled around and took a defensive fighting stance. Jarvis stood there, cringing, with his paws floating up to cover his face.

"Take it easy!" he exclaimed.

"Don't sneak up on me like that!" she retorted. "You almost gave me a heart attack!"

"Sorry," said Jarvis, looking abashed. "I didn't find anything good in the pantry. The only thing in there was about a million tons of canned sardines."

"Eww," said Bernie, wrinkling her nose. "Maybe that's why the ship sank. The crew was sick of eating sardines and blew a hole in the side of the ship so they could leave."

They both laughed, causing a spray of bubbles.

"Well, I got the battery charging. It's already at thirty percent! Come closer and I'll get your goggles working again," said Bernie.

Jarvis swam over. Bernie took the battery out of her pocket and held the metal rod near his Soggies. Like Bernie, his eyes widened in surprise when they rebooted and offered him the enhanced-reality view of the ocean.

"Better, huh?" asked Bernie.

"Yes and no!" said Jarvis nervously. "I kind of liked not having to see so much." He pointed at a large manta ray that, from their point of view, appeared to be the size of a stealth bomber.

As they made their way back to the opening, Bernie noticed that Jarvis's swimming had improved a bit.

"Hey, Jarvie, you're getting better," she said as they swam out of the hole together and started toward the *Cheese Dip*.

"I still don't like it," he said. "But I'm kind of getting the hang of not panicking as much."

"Well, I'm proud of you, y'know?" said Bernie. "You faced your fear."

"Bernie?" said Jarvis.

"What?"

"B-Bernie!" shouted Jarvis.

"What!"

Bernie whipped around and was face-to-face with the reason for Jarvis's fears. Swimming toward them rapidly was something she'd really, really hoped they wouldn't see. It was huge, with a long, pointed snout and rows and rows of razor-sharp teeth.

A barracuda!

"Frog feet!" shouted Bernie. Jarvis didn't need to be told twice. They both kicked their heels together and rocketed

toward their sub. The Soggies displayed the distance to the *Cheese Dip*: 125 yards.

When she'd first tried them on, Captain Crumb had told Bernie that the frog feet were fast—fast enough to outswim most predators. But the barracuda chasing them must have been exceptionally hungry, because it was almost catching up!

"Evasive maneuvers!" shouted Bernie. "You go left and I'll go right! We have to confuse it!"

Jarvis was too scared to answer but did exactly as she ordered. They both veered off in opposite directions, their flippers whirring like hummingbird wings as they tried to lose the ferocious predator.

The barracuda's hunter instinct reacted almost immediately. After the briefest pause, it shot after Jarvis—who was clearly the less skilled swimmer.

"Ahhhh!" Jarvis yelled.

I have to do something! Bernie felt herself starting to panic and mentally kicked herself with her frog feet for not taking a Jellyfisher with them. She was helpless!

Then she remembered that the Soggies could do a lot more than she'd been using them for. Captain Crumb had mentioned that they had a multitude of options. Could there be a solution for this?

She tapped the side of the goggles, just like she'd done

countless times before on her original Mouse Watch pair.
An electronic female voice replied, "Ready."

"We're being attacked by a barracuda!" Bernie shouted.

"Accessing database," said the calm voice. A split
second later, it replied, "Orca option?"

Bernie had no idea what "Orca option" meant, but it
had to be better than doing nothing.

"Yes, yes, do it now!"

Her goggles flashed bright green. Then, to her amazement, a life-size hologram of a killer whale materialized
about twenty feet from her. The goggles made a rapid
assessment of the barracuda's trajectory, projecting a tar-
geting crosshair and distance measurement on the fast
predator. Jarvis was screaming and desperately swerving
in erratic patterns, all the time just narrowly avoiding the
snapping jaws that were chomping at his frog feet.

The holo-Orca torpedoed after the barracuda.

As it gave chase, Bernie was reminded of the feature
on her Watcher goggles that allowed agents to take on the
appearance of someone else. The disguises were so con-
vincingly real that she'd been fooled by Digit, a double
agent who had betrayed the Mouse Watch.

It turned out that the hologram of the Orca was just as
convincing. Killer whales are one of the few creatures that
barracudas are terrified of. When the predator fish caught

sight of the gigantic black-and-white shape hurtling toward it, its eyes grew as wide as sand dollars and it immediately gave up chasing Jarvis. In a panic, the barracuda shot off as quickly as its fins could carry it, speeding away through the water even faster than it had been chasing them.

When it was only a speck on the watery horizon, the computer voice said, "Danger averted."

Relief washed over Bernie as the Orca hologram faded away. It had worked so well that she made a mental note not to forget it for the future. Had she known about that feature back when the *Cheese Dip* was first under attack, maybe Octavia would never have come to the rescue and they wouldn't have had to deal with her.

The thought made Bernie kick herself for not thinking of it. Even though Octavia was helping them find Catlantis—and getting them one step closer to the SS *Moon* and the Milk Saucer—she was convinced that, with a little more effort and time, they would have been able to figure out how to get there by themselves.

Bernie immediately swam to Jarvis, who was huddled next to a big piece of coral, trembling from head to foot.

"Are you okay?" said Bernie.

"I—I—I—" Jarvis stuttered.

"You're not hurt? It doesn't look like it bit you," said Bernie.

"I—I—I—" Jarvis continued.

"You what?" asked Bernie.

"I . . . never want to go into the ocean again!" Jarvis spluttered. "I'm done! That's it!"

And with that, he swam off in the direction of the *Cheese Dip* as fast as he could. Even though Bernie prided herself on being brave, she couldn't blame him one bit as she turned and followed him.

Sometimes, Bernie thought, *our worst fears actually do come true in real life.*

Once back inside the safety of the submarine, Jarvis made a beeline for his cabin and slammed the door. Bernie sighed. They had survived that disaster, but her anxiety about Catlantis was only growing stronger.

The encounter with the barracuda had rattled her. If it wasn't for her last-minute quick thinking, Jarvis would be fish food.

I only hope he'd do the same for me if I got attacked by a cat, she thought.

CHAPTER 17

Jarvis stayed in his cabin for a while. When he finally emerged, it seemed as if facing the worst fear of his life (twice in two days) was having a lasting effect on him.

"Well, at least now I know," he confessed. "It was every bit as bad as I'd feared, but you know what? I survived!"

Bernie patted him on the back. "You sure did," she said. But inwardly, she was dreading facing her *own* worst fear. Even the idea of swimming with sharks and barracudas, as scary as that was, didn't hold a candle to where they were headed.

I hope I can pull it together as well as Jar, she thought. She was plagued with visions of herself huddled in the corner of her room at home, muttering about tabbies and Siamese, having been tossed out of the Mouse Watch for acting like a total coward in Catlantis. If she refused to leave the sub, that was exactly what would happen.

They'd throw her out for sure.

At least Jarvis faced his fear and went underwater even though he was dreading it, she thought. That alone took an amazing amount of courage.

She could appreciate what he did more than ever, now that she was experiencing stomach-churning terror herself.

The fully charged battery was reinstalled. Seconds later, the sub was back to total operating power. And, whether it was perfect timing or something else, that ended up being precisely the moment Octavia decided to show up again in her kraken submarine.

She initiated ship-to-ship video transmission. The crew gathered in the command center as the two captains spoke to each other from their respective bridges.

"I'm so sorry that I wasn't there to help with the eel," said Octavia. "I needed to go on ahead and announce your visit to the empress of Catlantis. She's delighted that you're coming, and is especially looking forward to meeting the young agents, Jarvis Slinktail and Bernadette Skampersky."

Bernie cringed. She hated being called Bernadette. Her mother usually used her full name when she was in big trouble. Octavia must have found out somehow that it was her full name, and Bernie felt her distrust for the mouse pirate growing even stronger.

"No worries at all, ma'am. Crisis solved," said Captain Crumb. Bernie noticed that he didn't make any mention of the dangerous mission she and Jarvis had accomplished in order to save the sub. She would have liked him to brag about her heroism a little bit, just to annoy Octavia.

"Well, if you'll just follow me then," said Octavia smoothly. "We'll be at Catlantis within the hour."

The screen winked off and Crumb turned to the others in the command center. "Follow that kraken!"

The SS *Cheese Dip* wheeled about and followed the massive mechanical creature as it headed west, navigating easily through the stiff current. The water had become more turbulent as the monsoon, as predicted, churned above the waves.

Bernie spent the remainder of the hour alone in her cabin. Her watch said that there was five and a half hours to go on their mission. This would have worried her more if she wasn't so preoccupied with her terrible fear of Catlantis.

Jarvis, feeling much less worried about being in the sub now that he'd faced far worse outside of it, had reclaimed both his Tabasco sauce from the kitchens and, with it, his old appetite. For whatever reason, he didn't share any of Bernie's anxieties about Catlantis. Even though he knew it might be dangerous, he seemed able to face this particular challenge in spite of his old fear of water.

I guess it all goes back to childhood, thought Bernie. *Ever since my brother, my greatest fear was rats. But Jarvis helped me get over that. Cats were always my second great fear. Water was Jarvis's.*

What I wouldn't give for all this to be over, she thought.

She leafed through a *Mega Mouse* comic book but couldn't really focus on it. Then she tried closing her eyes, but every time she did, visions of yellow cat eyes startled her.

Finally, an announcement came through the scuppers. "Catlantis off the port bow!"

Bernie rushed from her cabin and peered out the porthole window. Through the hazy water she could see several giant glass domes on the ocean floor. Inside them were elegant Egyptian-style pyramids and obelisks. If she hadn't known that it was a home for cats, she would have been dying to explore it.

Learning from her mistake on the battery-charging mission, Bernie made absolutely sure she had her Jellyfisher with her. She kept the weapon stowed safely, near at hand in her aqua suit pocket.

She was so nervous that her stomach was churning like a washing machine. She thought she might throw up at any second.

She felt a paw on her shoulder and looked up to see Jarvis smiling kindly down at her.

"You were there for me, now let me be there for you."

Bernie nodded gratefully and placed her little paw on top of his. Having her best friend there made a big difference.

The SS *Cheese Dip* followed the *Medusa* down to a docking area near the largest dome. They could see through the glass but, to her surprise, Bernie's goggles didn't display the usual information tags on what she saw inside.

"Jar, do your Soggies show you anything about those buildings?" asked Bernie, pointing to the Egyptian-style structures.

"Huh. No," said Jarvis. "This place is completely off the map—or something."

"Or something," echoed Bernie nervously.

Minutes later, the hatch was lifted on the submarine. Bernie was surprised to see that a tightly sealed glass tunnel had been fitted to the SS *Cheese Dip*, allowing the passengers to step directly from the sub into the air-locked kingdom of cats.

Bernie followed the rest of the crew onto a beautiful green-and-gold boat dock and stared around in awe.

Egyptian obelisks with hieroglyphic symbols stretched high into the air. She counted five great pyramids with a giant, sphinxlike statue in the center of the city. Bernie noticed the sphinx had a cat's face on it instead of a human's.

But it makes sense in this place, I guess, she thought with a shiver.

The air was clean but very dry, and the temperature was quite warm. At first, Bernie wondered if it was regulated by some kind of thermostat, but then she spotted small, glowing orbs like stars decorating the tops of the pyramids. When she looked up at them, she could feel heat on her face and whiskers.

They have their own mini suns!

It was a relief to be out of the sub and breathing in the fresh air, but Bernie couldn't help wondering where the air came from. Was it generated inside of the massive dome? Pumped in from somewhere up above? How it was produced, she had no idea, but this strange underwater city looked exactly like books she had read in school about ancient Egypt.

"It's terrifying and incredible at the same time," she whispered.

"Yeah," Jarvis whispered back. "I get what you mean."

As they made their way down the docks to the sandy shoreline, an entire city stretched out before them with colorful green-and-gold awnings over shops selling anything a cat might wish for, from multicolored feathered toys to baskets of fresh catnip.

Then, in spite of the heat, Bernie suddenly turned cold. She could see something moving toward them, glittering gold in the light. As it drew closer, she realized it was a golden throne, and to her horror, it was carried by four of the largest cats Bernie had ever seen. Sitting on the throne was an elegant tabby with long orange fur. She wore the headdress of a pharaoh. As she grew closer, her glittering green eyes struck terror in Bernie's heart.

Bernie tried hard to suppress the scream that wanted so badly to come out.

This was clearly an important cat and was, like everything else Bernie had seen so far, both beautiful and horrifying. She watched with terrified fascination as the regal kitty motioned for her guards to set the throne down directly in front of the newcomers. The burliest of the four cats announced, "Her Royal Majesty, the Empress Cleopatra Marshmallow Fluffyface the Third."

The tabby slowly maneuvered her massive bulk to the ground, and then walked over to them with a surprisingly dainty stride, a welcoming smile on her feline features.

"Welcome, my small friends. Welcome to Catlantis! You may simply address me as 'Empress' if you pre-furrrrrr."

CHAPTER 18

Bernie's knees trembled. She stared up at the empress, who towered over her. She didn't know how to react. She had greeted them so nicely, but she was also downright terrifying!

Don't eat me, please, please, please. . . .

"Please, follow me to the pounce-il chamber," said the empress, clapping her paws together. She climbed gracefully back on her throne.

Because her paws were so velvety, they hardly made a sound. However, the guards must have had excellent hearing, for they immediately picked up the litter and carried their massive queen toward a low, gold-trimmed building nearby. The mice (and rat) had no choice but to follow.

Bernie didn't know what to expect and tried her best to keep from envisioning all kinds of horrible traps that might be waiting for them inside the pounce-il chamber. She hid a little behind Jarvis as they walked. Jarvis, for a change, was relatively calm. Since brushing up against the horrors of the ocean, he'd found a little more courage.

However, once they stepped into the richly decorated pounce-il chamber, a cylindrically shaped building with historical paintings of cats decorating the walls, Bernie was immensely relieved to find that there were no cats waiting to pounce. Instead, they were led to a lounge area with luxurious cushioned couches and were each given a golden goblet with chilled seaberry juice.

The cups, of course, were cat-size, but Bernie was able to climb up the side of hers and sip carefully from the rim. Her mouth had been dry with fear, and the delicious gulp of sweet and spicy seaberry juice cooled her parched throat. She caught just a hint of saltiness and something that tasted a little like plum. It was a bit briny and surprisingly refreshing.

As the cool drink slid down her throat, for a split second her raging fear was reduced to a low simmer. Being greeted so warmly was a positive step!

The empress sat languidly on her gold-winged throne, observing the group with an amused smile.

Captain Crumb stepped forward. Bernie noticed that he looked a little uncomfortable and was trying his best at being well mannered and cordial. He gripped his battered old sea captain's hat in his paws and kept his eyes slightly lowered as a sign of respect.

"Er . . . greetings, Your Royal Cat-ness. Your tremendous size is very . . . tremendous. Tremendously impressive, I mean, and . . . well, you see . . . well . . . we've come to ask you for your help. Er . . . it's like this. . . ."

"Stop." The empress interrupted Crumb's request, holding up a big paw and staring at him coolly. "We are bored."

Crumb stared, dumbfounded.

"Wh-wh-what?" he stammered.

Octavia then stepped forward and, after gently pushing Crumb aside, bowed with her paws outstretched and her tail lowered so that it was touching the floor.

"O truly tremendous one. O living goddess of feline majesty! Cat of cats, and purrrrfection purrrsonified."

Bernie noticed that Octavia rolled her *r*'s when she said "purrrrfection purrrsonified." This seemed to please the empress no end. She purred quietly in response and seemed to bask in the flattery.

"As you know, I, Octavia Gillywhisk, have always endeavored to please Your Highness with not a single thought of my own regard."

Yeah, right, thought Bernie. She doubted Octavia ever had a thought that *wasn't* of her own regard.

"And as my ineloquent and rrrrather crass associate

hasn't yet had the pleasure of experiencing your glory before, he must be forrrrgiven for his rather clumsy request," she continued.

The empress seemed to agree with the way Octavia was handling things. She lifted her chin and appeared even more imperious. Bernie caught Crumb glowering at Octavia. He wasn't used to being embarrassed in front of his crew. All he'd done was to try and be direct. Why did Octavia have to make fun of him? And why did this fat, fluffy feline deserve all this pomp and circumstance? She was scary in theory, but now that Bernie was seeing her up close, she thought she also seemed like a big, spoiled baby.

"But," Octavia continued, "even in his primitive awkwardness, what he says is true. He and his pathetic crew of rodents are desperate for your mercy." Crumb visibly cringed as Octavia spoke. "They are on a mission of tremendous importance that, if accomplished, would mean more safety and security for your glorious kingdom. I humbly beg of you to consider his request."

Octavia finished by flourishing her paws and extending herself in an even deeper bow.

Oh brother, thought Bernie.

A long moment passed while the empress considered the request. "You arrrre most welcome to stay and rrrrrest for the night," she purred. "However, Catlantis doesn't intervene in top-dweller affairs. We prefurrrr to keep to ourselves."

She slid her glittering emerald eyes over the entire crew until she spotted Bernie and Jarvis. Bernie had been watching her every move like a hawk and felt her spine tingle with fear when she saw the emerald eyes lock on to her.

"By the goddess Bastet, I didn't rrrrrealize that the two young agents who saved that kitten in a tree were here. You arrrre especially welcome," purred the fluffy queen.

"H-h-how did you know about that?" Bernie squeaked.

The empress laughed, an effect that caused her entire belly to wobble beneath the thick coat of golden fur. "Why, all cats use telepathy. But you knew that, of course."

She added this statement like it was common knowledge, but Bernie had no idea what she was talking about. *Cats communicate telepathically?* It kind of made sense in a scary, not altogether unexpected way. Bernie had always felt that there was something creepy about cats. Of course they had weird psychic powers.

Bernie tried unsuccessfully to suppress a shudder. The empress noticed and clucked her tongue in sympathy.

"Oh, you're cold, you purrrrr little morsel," she said. She turned to Crumb and Octavia and raised a velvety paw as if uttering a royal decree.

"Because these honored heroes who saved one of ourrrr own are now among us, we have decided that you and yourrrr entire crew will stay as our special guests in the Pyramid of the Sun. It will certainly warm you up. My guards will show you the way. And tonight, we'll hold a delicious welcome feast in yourrrr honor."

"Sounds good, I'm starving," said Jarvis. The empress and her attendants chuckled, giving one another glances that seemed to indicate they found their new friends humorous and delightful.

She clapped her massive paws again, and the two burly guards, one a muscle-bound black cat and the other a gray tomcat who was missing an eye, stepped forward and motioned for everyone to follow. Before they left, the empress added, "The fact that yourrrr two brave companions laid their lives on the line to help a cat—your sworn enemy—is not lost on us." She stared at the captain for a long time, until he grew uncomfortable under her glittering emerald gaze. "I can, of course, rrrrread your mind, Captain. You arrre looking for a map to the SS *Moon*, yes?"

Crumb stared back at her with a dumbfounded expression. "How do you do that?" he said. She waved off the question and smiled.

"As I said before, we cats have special powerrrrs you little mice cannot possibly conceive of."

"If you know of its location, we'd be happy to pay you whatever price you ask," Crumb said eagerly.

"The map is kept in a place that only a rrroyal cat

knows, so don't get any ideas about trying to find it without purrrmission," she said firmly. Then her gaze softened. "I do believe we have what you're looking furrr. But I must warn you, the SS *Moon* is purrr-tected. You'd do betterrrr to avoid it. My psychic powers furrrr-see much trouble for you ahead—much, much trouble, I'm afraid. But we can discuss these things later. Furrr now, please enjoy the hospitality of Catlantis."

The cat and Octavia exchanged glances. The empress motioned for her to stay. "Octavia, you will rrrrremain. I have a separate matter to discuss with you."

"I am Your Majesty's humble servant," said Octavia.

"Humble servant"? Oh, come on! Bernie wondered what that was all about. Why was Octavia staying behind?

She hazarded a quick glance at Captain Crumb. The captain had evidently overcome his embarrassment from Octavia's speech and now looked cautiously optimistic.

He didn't seem bothered that Octavia and the empress were staying back to speak privately, but it only made Bernie more suspicious of her possible duplicity. She didn't tell the group this, of course, as they followed the royal guards out of the pounce-il chamber and into the bustling streets of Catlantis.

I guess Crumb thinks it's safe, thought Bernie. *But does he really know for sure?*

It all felt like a major delay they couldn't afford. They

had already encountered so many obstacles. Who knew where the R.A.T.S. were! They could already have made it to the Milk Saucer!

She glanced at her watch. Just a little over four hours left on the countdown clock!

As Bernie and the rest of the crew walked down the golden-paved streets, she thought about how seeing the cats close up was terrifying, but she also had to admit that the empress had been much, much friendlier than she'd initially envisioned. She'd thought they would be colder, or even try to attack the crew of mice, but they hadn't. Perhaps Bernie had misjudged them. She'd been known to do that kind of thing before. After all, she'd misjudged Jarvis—and now he was her best friend.

Maybe there's no harm in enjoying myself a little, Bernie thought.

The pyramids looked a lot closer to the docks than they actually were. Bernie couldn't help wondering how Catlantis had come to be. It looked ancient, but something about it felt . . . off, like it had been constructed by cats for cats. As Bernie looked around, she realized the tall buildings reminded her of the carpeted cat-scratching towers sold in pet stores. They were constructed of sandstone and had countless round entrances to dark interiors in case a cat needed privacy. They were also covered in deep scratches, like on a scratching post. But these looked almost artful, and on further inspection Bernie realized they depicted various pictures of cat deities. There were also sunny platforms and seating areas for cats to perch upon and look down on everyone else from a great height.

As they walked, Bernie's mind was working overtime. *How is it all possible? Is Catlantis an island that sank? Is it maintained by magic?* she wondered. *Or is there some strange science behind all this?*

The city was bright and warm, as if it were a sunny day in July. She had to admit that she was very comfortable. She wanted to ask one of the cat guards her questions, but because they looked so serious, she felt like she didn't want to risk it.

The group continued to follow the big guard cats through the desert marketplace, and Bernie noticed she and Jarvis attracted a lot of smiles and whispers. Maybe these Catlantis cats had never seen a mouse or a rat before. Or maybe they had heard of their daring kitten rescue. They all stared with open fascination at the two unusual creatures.

The group made their way through a big open-air market, and Bernie couldn't help noticing that most of the food for sale was fish. It gave her a bit of comfort.

Maybe eating mice is a land-cat thing, she reasoned. *Perhaps eating fish is all they've ever known.*

Jarvis, meanwhile, shared none of Bernie's anxiety. Since there didn't seem to be any immediate threat from the cats, he spent his time admiring all the unusual sights in the market, commenting on the funny-looking cat toys that, up close, weren't made of feathers but instead were made of ingeniously designed, brightly colored seaweed strands.

"Look at this," said Jarvis. Bernie looked at the toy fishing pole he was pointing to. The "fish" at the bottom of the line was a toy in the shape of an octopus that bobbed playfully up and down. The tentacles were made of seaweed.

"Cool," said Bernie. Then, leaning close to Jarvis, she whispered, "If it keeps those cats playing with seafood rather than us, then I'm all for it. I just want to stay focused, get the map, get out of here as fast as we can, and find the SS *Moon*."

"You heard the empress; she said she'll help us," said Jarvis. "But in the meantime, maybe we can enjoy ourselves a teeny bit."

Kittens frolicked and played with giant balls of yarn that rolled down the paved streets. They seemed innocently curious when they saw Bernie and Jarvis walking by, and not a single one of them showed any aggression whatsoever.

I only wish they were like this back home, thought Bernie.

At one point, a friendly vendor came out and offered Bernie and Jarvis each a delicate cheese pastry. "Furrr the young guests," she purred.

Bernie sniffed it and then, not wanting to seem rude, decided to take a bite. It was delicious.

"Thank you very much," she said. "You're very kind."

The vendor seemed pleased and chuckled to herself.

"Aren't you adorrrrable!" she purred, pointing down at Bernie as if she were an exceptionally bright child. "I can't wait to enjoy you betterrrr at the welcome feast," she purred again.

Enjoy me? Bernie thought. *That seems like a strange way to put it. I guess it's a cat thing.*

"Sounds great," said Bernie. "We'll talk more then!"

The old cat laughed and patted Bernie on the head. Bernie didn't particularly like being talked to like she was two years old, but she didn't want to argue and risk angering the cats. Better to be given treats than to *be* the treat.

Finally, the group followed the guards into the most spectacular dwelling Bernie had seen yet.

She'd mistakenly assumed that inside of the pyramid would have been a series of dark tunnels leading to solemn, empty stone cells without windows. But when she stepped inside, the sight took her breath away.

She stood in a bright, cavernous room with soaring

ceilings. Another artificial sun, something made by cat science or sorcery, glowed at the apex, filling the entire area with warm sunlight.

"Is that a real sun?" wondered Bernie aloud.

To her surprise, one of the cat guards next to her actually replied. "In ancient times, ourrrr ancestors learned the secret of the Prometheus flame. Ourrr magicians used alchemy to create mini-suns after the great flood."

"So, Catlantis sank into the ocean?" asked Bernie.

"Yes," said the guard. "But it was because we decided to make it so. Our ancestorrrrs built the great dome and created the flood that brought us below. We cats neverrrr do anything that we don't want to. We chose this life because we found life among the top dwellers dull and uninspired. Some of them werrre even trying to domesticate us! That could never be. Mortals. Stupid, ignorant mortals."

He trailed off with a look of extreme annoyance on his face. Bernie decided that asking anything else might be a bad idea. She'd probably pushed her luck too far already.

She gazed at the tall balconies that rose in ascending tiers along the slanted pyramid walls. On each one, cats lounged on golden couches, lapping from golden bowls of milk. Bernie wondered how they got it. Maybe they had it delivered from the surface?

It was obviously a favorite dish, and the entire room

vibrated with the contented purrs of its feline inhabitants.

"Your rrrrooms are here," purred the cat guard nearest to Bernie. He showed her to the first of two very spacious royal rooms. Bernie noticed that beautiful hieroglyphic art decorated the walls and that the entire room had an open view of the city below. There were also lots of sparkly, dangly things hanging from various places on the ceiling for cat occupants to bat around when bored.

"Please, make yourrrrselves comfortable," said the cat in a soft, low voice. "We will be purrr-viding room service shortly. Consider yourselves fortunate to be blessed by the empress, tiny friends."

As he left, Bernie had to admit to herself that maybe all of her fears had been for nothing at all.

"This is pretty nice," she murmured.

But it was tough to enjoy it when she also thought about the urgency of their mission. They needed to get to the Milk Saucer. What if the R.A.T.S. were already there? How could they lounge around like the cats that lived here when the fate of the world might be at stake!

"They're bringing us all kinds of food!" said Jarvis, entering the room. "They even said I could order whatever I wanted! Pretty great, huh?"

Bernie nodded. "Yeah, it's so different from what I thought it would be. But, Jar, we can't stay here. We've got to get to that shipwreck as soon as possible!"

"But we have to eat, don't we?" complained Jarvis. "I'm totally starving! That weird juice they gave us hardly made a dent in my appetite."

They were interrupted by a knock on the door. Bernie and Jarvis exchanged glances, and Bernie tentatively said, "Come in." A matronly cat with white fur and flowing white robes pushed a tray laden with delicious-looking fruit—three plump, juicy grapes and an entire strawberry!—and a mountain of exotic pastry crumbs.

For Bernie and Jarvis it was a feast!

"Ah, my young herrrroes," said the cat. "You both look half-starved! Please, help yourrrrselves to all you want. I'll get in trouble with Her Majesty if you don't eat at least half of what's here."

Bernie's mouth watered as she stared at the tower of delicious treats. She didn't think that there was any possible way in the world the two of them could come close to eating even half of what was there. As the elderly cat bustled out of the room, Bernie turned to Jarvis with a grin.

"Jar, I know you're always hungry, but even *you* can't eat this much. . . ." Her voice trailed off when she realized he wasn't next to her.

"Jarvie?"

"Mmmmm! Oh man . . . this is amazing!"

Then, looking up, Bernie saw that Jarvis was perched

on top of the mountain of food, tucking into one of the grapes with a knife and fork.

"Well, I guess if anyone could eat their way through this, it would be you," Bernie said, grinning. Jarvis was sprinkling his Tabasco sauce with liberal abandon over everything on the platter, even the fruit!

"Hey, take it easy with that stuff. I don't want any on mine!" she said, protectively holding the strawberry out of her friend's reach.

"Oh . . . (munch, munch) . . . but . . . Oh! It's all so . . . (munch, munch) . . . good!" Jarvis said with his cheeks so full they puffed out like balloons. Bernie carved out a little section of the mountain for herself and, using the good manners she'd been raised with, ate politely.

Jarvis was right. The food was expertly prepared with exotic flavors and unusual, delicate spices. Bernie wasn't sure, but she could have sworn that one of the pastry crumbs had been sprinkled with something strange. Was it catnip?

But it was all very delicious and, once she started, she found it very, very hard to stop!

Soon, the mouse and rat had collapsed on the fluffy cat bed and were reclining on silk pillows.

"I can't eat another bite," moaned Bernie.

"I can't . . . resist eating one more!" said Jarvis. He cut off a piece of the remaining grape. Before it reached his mouth, he hit it with a couple of drops of Tabasco.

"Seriously. On a grape?" said Bernie.

Jarvis was so full he could barely chew. But between mouthfuls, he managed, "It makes everything better."

"Then how come you didn't use it when we were on Octavia's ship?" Bernie asked pointedly.

Jarvis paused to swallow. Then he said, "That was different. I wanted to make a good impression."

"I think you're wasting your time there," said Bernie. "I don't trust her one bit."

"Why?" said Jarvis. "She was nice to us. Sure, she might have been a little bit arrogant—"

"A little bit?" interrupted Bernie. "Yeah, that's an understatement. But I'm bothered more by the fact that she charged for helping us. I mean, who does that?"

Jarvis shrugged. "Someone who is looking out for themselves, I guess."

"Exactly," said Bernie. "And those who are only out for themselves can't always be trusted. I think that a mouse like that might double-cross us."

"Whoa!" said Jarvis. "You can't be serious!"

"I am," said Bernie, pouting. "There's something fishy . . . no pun intended."

"Well, you might be right," said Jarvis thoughtfully. "I thought it was a little suspicious when she said she found everyone's luggage but yours."

"Right?" said Bernie, sitting up. "That was weird."

Jarvis nodded. "We should keep our eye on her. And by the way, the only reason I was having fun talking to her was because she was kind of a tech head like me."

"I get that, but lives are on the line here," said Bernie. "We can't automatically trust someone like that and share tech secrets. Even if she was once part of the Mouse Watch, she isn't anymore. It's important, Jar."

Jarvis stared at her until Bernie got uncomfortable.

"What?" she said.

"I'm just looking at you and trying to figure out whether you see what I see," said Jarvis.

"Oh? And what's that?" asked Bernie.

"I see somebody who has been the most loyal good friend I've ever had and who I'm gonna stick by forever. You're the greatest Mouse Watch agent I've ever seen," said Jarvis with a shrug.

Bernie felt a warm glow spread through her insides.

"Thanks for saying that," said Bernie shyly.

"No problem," said Jarvis with a grin. "It's true. You totally faced your fears to be here and also helped me face mine. I think you're awesome."

"Really?" said Bernie.

"Really," said Jarvis.

There was a happy pause, the kind that is a little awkward because nobody is saying anything, but it was also special because both of them knew what the other one was thinking.

"Hey, Jarvie?" said Bernie.

"Don't call me that. What?" said Jarvis.

"My stomach really hurts."

Jarvis chuckled. "Mine too. Maybe we should see if they have some medicine for indigestion. Wanna see if we can find that nice old cat from the kitchens?"

"Not really," said Bernie. "These cats are all being super nice, but they still freak me out. However, I feel like I'm going to pop, so let's go."

On their way, they asked directions from the numerous lounging felines about where the kitchens were. Like before, the cats were all very nice and helpful, and many of them commented on how cute and funny Bernie and Jarvis were and how much they looked forward to having them at the feast.

"They're almost too nice," said Bernie.

"Better than the alternative, right?" said Jarvis.

"Yeah, but I mean I know I sound so suspicious of everyone these days, but the way those cats are acting creeps me out. Cats are cats, Jar. They have instincts! They like eating mice!"

"Yeah, but rats all get a bad reputation and it's not always true. What if you're just being judgy?"

"I'm not, though," said Bernie. But secretly, she wondered if her fear of cats was the reason for her distrust.

I can't help it, she thought. *Something seems definitely off.*

They followed the instructions they were given, and after navigating the pyramid they found a side tunnel with a hieroglyphic cat holding a tray of food and an arrow pointing to the kitchens.

When they found the vast, impressive room they were surprised to see that it was empty.

"Hellooo?" called Bernie.

No answer.

"Let's look around. Maybe there's a medical kit around somewhere."

They started to search the area, looking in drawers and shelves for anything that might look like medicine. Bernie had just about given up looking and was starting to battle a severe case of heartburn, when she saw a big book lying open on the kitchen chopping block.

She tried to make out the hieroglyphic symbols, but suddenly had trouble focusing her eyes. They were growing heavy and her vision was really blurry. She glanced at Jarvis and saw that he was yawning and curled up with a big spatula for a pillow.

"Jar . . . I think there might have been something in . . . in our food. . . ."

But she wasn't even able to finish what she was about

to say because it felt like a big, warm blanket was covering her whole body. She was powerless to fight the urge to fall asleep. She noticed the big book lying open and curled up between the soft pages.

Through bleary eyes, Bernie looked down at her new bed and saw pictures of seasonings and spices. There was a photograph of a cat sprinkling salt over two small pieces of meat simmering on a hot stove.

A *cookbook?* thought Bernie.

Everything faded slowly, and then the world around her turned to black.

CHAPTER 19

"Jarvis, Jarvis! Wake up!" shouted Bernie. She'd opened her eyes to a horrifying sight! Arranged in neat little rows and tied down with twine on a huge baking pan was the whole SS *Cheese Dip* crew, including Captain Crumb. They were all covered with sticky, gooey sauce. Bernie was the only one awake! "Wake up!" she yelled again. "We're not guests at this feast! We're the MAIN COURSE!"

The fishy smell of the sauce stung her nostrils. Although it made her stomach turn, she was grateful. The fact that the chef had left them to marinate meant that they had a small window of time to escape!

Jarvis finally opened his eyes. When he saw what was happening, he let out a loud squeak of fright.

"Shhh!" hissed Bernie. "We can't risk them coming back."

"They're gonna . . . gonna . . ."

"Cook us," said Bernie. "I knew it was too good to be true! But we can't let that happen. Do you still have the Lazer Blazer I gave you? Please tell me you didn't leave it on the sub."

"I do!" said Jarvis, remembering the gadget Bernie had given him as a present earlier. Thankfully, the way the cords were arranged around his body, he had enough room to reach his paw into his hoodie pocket. The Lazer Blazer burned through the twine holding them captive.

Seconds later, both he and Bernie were free.

"That is one of the nicest gifts anyone has ever given me," said Jarvis. "Thank you, Bernie. Thank you, thank you, THANK YOU!"

"Okay, let's free the others and get out of here!" said Bernie. They set about waking up and untying the ten crew members. Captain Crumb woke up with a splutter.

"By cheddar, we've been double-crossed!" he exclaimed. He looked around at the crew suspiciously. "And Octavia's the only one who's not here!"

"Glad you noticed," said Bernie. She had, of course, noticed right away that the captain of the *Medusa* wasn't marinating along with the rest of the group. Crumb glowered as Jarvis cut through the twine with his Lazer Blazer.

"We've got to retrieve the map and get back to the ship," Crumb said. Turning to Jarvis, he added, "Okay,

Slinktail, they tell me you're the best at solving riddles. Where would these cats hide what we're looking for?"

"Sir . . . I . . . I'm not a detective," spluttered Jarvis.

"Wait, Jarvie, you kind of are," said Bernie. "Think of it like a puzzle. What have you seen since we've been here? You have the best memory of anyone I know. What are the clues to solving where the map is located? Have you seen or heard anything suspicious?"

Jarvis furrowed his brow, thinking. He got that faraway gaze Bernie knew meant he was concentrating his hardest. After a long moment, he sighed and shrugged his shoulders.

"There's only one thing that struck me as odd. It might not mean anything, but . . ."

"Go on," encouraged Crumb. "Anything could help, Slinktail."

"Well, when you asked the empress about the map, she said, 'The map is kept in a place that only a royal cat knows.'"

"But that doesn't help at all," growled Crumb. "We're not royal cats."

"Ah, but if you think of the words a little differently, it might mean that it's kept in a royal cat's NOSE."

"Of course!" said Bernie. "Aren't sphinxes symbolic of royalty? What if the map is in the nose of the cat sphinx in the center of the city?"

"I suppose it's the best clue we've got," said Crumb, pounding his fist into his paw. "Let's get out of here!"

Bernie was thankful that cats, by nature, loved open windows and doors and hated being confined. It made it much easier to escape the kitchen. The toughest part, since they were covered in fish sauce, was avoiding being sniffed out. Bernie was afraid, as they made their way back through the pyramid, that the cats might pick up their scent.

But to her surprise, there was no one around. It was the hottest part of the day and all the cats in the city were in their rooms taking catnaps, resting up before the nighttime feast to come.

The timing couldn't have been better!

Bernie glanced at her watch. Only two hours and twelve minutes left to finish the mission!

We'll never make it!

But even as the thought entered her head, Bernie thought about her friends—Jarvis, the crew, and Captain Crumb—and decided that, by cheddar, she was going to try!

As they left the pyramid, one of the guards stirred briefly in his sleep, his nose twitching as the tiny troop of mice snuck by. Bernie's breath caught in her throat! The entire group froze. None of them moved a muscle for a long moment. But then, thankfully, he sniffed a little and settled back into a deep sleep, and they were able to continue sneaking out, emerging unscathed onto the hot Catlantis streets.

"Okay, all we have is a Lazer Blazer, a Jellyfisher, our whiskers, and our wits," Crumb said. "So, here's what we're going to do. I'll go with Slinktail and Skampersky. You lot go back to the *Cheese Dip* and get her ready to sail at a moment's notice. If we manage to find that map, we're going to want to get the Havarti out of here."

The crew saluted and dashed off toward the docks.

"Let's go," said Crumb. The three scampered off in the direction of the sphinx. Bernie's heart raced with fear and excitement as they ran.

What if we don't find the map in time and the cats wake up? What if we find the map and we're still not in time to stop the R.A.T.S. from finding the Milk Saucer? What if we can't even find the map? What if Jarvis's "clue" is all wrong and there's nothing there?

This steady narrative kept running through her mind as they raced to the center of the city. But she forced herself to stay strong, fighting back those thoughts with other, more positive ones like, *You've got this, Bernie. This is the kind of adventure you live for!*

And it really did help her feel stronger to think that way. She realized that the positive thoughts mean more than the negative ones when you give them that power.

The three were so focused that none of them spoke

as they ran. Crumb's Navy peacoat flapped behind him as he ran, making the only sound on the eerily silent city streets. Bernie was pleasantly surprised to find that, probably because he was terrified, Jarvis had no trouble keeping up with them.

He's got more physical ability than he thinks, thought Bernie. *All he needed was the right motivation.*

After a solid bit of running, the three of them reached the massive front paws of the sphinx. There was a door right between them, in the center of the crouching feline's chest. It wasn't lost on Bernie that it would have been the worst place to be if the sphinx had been real. She would never intentionally stand between a cat's paws. It was like asking to be squished.

"Okay, keep your guard up," whispered Bernie. "Who knows what we might find inside."

Crumb nodded. "Good thinking, Skampersky. Stick close to me."

Upon entering, they were surprised to find that this place was much darker than the other buildings they'd been inside. There was no artificial sun, and everything seemed gloomy.

"Look," said Jarvis, pointing up. Bernie noticed that he had his Soggies on, and she cursed herself for being stupid. She slid hers down over her eyes and looked where he was pointing.

The goggles' night vision illuminated the room, and Bernie stifled a gasp when she saw what Jarvis was pointing at. There, on a higher level, surrounded by shelves containing dozens of ancient scrolls, were the empress and Octavia. They were bent over a table inspecting something and speaking in low voices.

Crumb held a finger to his whiskers and motioned for them to follow. Along the walls were the same cat ramps that they'd seen in the pyramid, and they crept up them as quietly as they could.

When they reached the top, Bernie saw that they were completely level with the sphinx's nose. They were surprised to see a small library nestled into one of the nostrils.

Cat knows. Cat NOSE. Jarvis is so clever, Bernie thought.

The empress and Octavia were focused on the big piece of papyrus stretched out on the table in front of them and didn't notice the mice hiding behind one of the nearby shelves.

That's got to be the map they're looking at, thought Bernie. She tilted her big ears toward the hushed conversation and heard Octavia say, "I've delivered you the mice. You're going to eat better than you have in ages. All I want in return is the *Cheese Dip* and this map. I invested a lot of money into that submarine and I want it back."

"We want more rodents," purred the empress. "We will

only give you the map if you promise to bring us more tasty, furrrrry morsels."

"But that's not what we agreed to," complained Octavia.

"Purrhaps not," said the empress. "But *we* are changing the agreement."

Bernie thought Octavia looked furious. "Okay, fine. I agree," she muttered through clenched teeth.

"Purrfect! We shall celebrate with a goblet of warm sea cow milk," said the empress. Bernie saw Octavia scowl. Drinking warm sea cow milk didn't sound like a great way to celebrate.

As the two of them moved over to a large cabinet to retrieve goblets, Bernie saw their chance. At a quick nod with Crumb and Jarvis, the three snuck to the table containing the map.

Everything was going perfectly. Bernie reached slowly and carefully for the map, hardly daring to breathe. She grasped the edges in her paws and slid it gently off the table, inch by inch. Finally, it was in her grasp!

But Bernie had been so focused on the map that she didn't see the small golden paperweight in the shape of a cat sitting next to her elbow. Just as she slid the map into her waiting paws, she bumped it.

It toppled back and forth for a minute.

Then the paperweight tipped, falling to the stone floor with a loud, heart-stopping CLANG!

The empress and Octavia wheeled around.

In a single, lightning-fast motion, Octavia drew a pistol from her belt and pointed it directly at Crumb.

"Well, hello, Captain. What an unpleasant surprise!"

"You're a traitor!" bellowed Crumb.

"A mouse has to make a living," said Octavia with a shrug. "Now order those mice to give me the map and the keys to the *Cheese Dip*. If you thought I made those modifications just to help you out, you were a fool. Kryptos will pay me top dollar for the Milk Saucer and I'll probably be able to sell him your sub for a nice profit, too."

Kryptos? Who's Kryptos? Bernie wondered. She thought the name sounded familiar, but she couldn't remember where she'd heard it before.

"You won't get away with this," growled Captain Crumb.

Bernie made sure she didn't.

Thinking fast, she grabbed the Jellyfisher in her pocket, turned it on, and threw it at Octavia.

It was a well-aimed shot. Octavia had quick reflexes, but they were not quite quick enough. She dodged, but the Jellyfisher hit her left leg and sent a zap of static electricity through her.

She dropped her pistol and screamed.

Captain Crumb didn't need a cue to know that it was time to hightail it out of there. "CHEESE IT!" he shouted.

Bernie gripped the map tightly and ran faster than she

ever had before, dashing toward the ramps that led out of the sphinx.

The empress pressed a crystal embedded in the wall, and a shrill, unearthly alarm that sounded like the wailing of a thousand cats assaulted their ears.

As they rushed out of the sphinx into the artificial afternoon sunlight, Bernie saw hordes of angry guards rushing toward them with spears leveled.

It was going to be close!

The three mice scampered as fast as they could, scurrying to outpace the Catlantis guards, who seemed to cover three times as much ground with every leaping stride.

The docks were in sight. The cats were drawing closer. Jarvis, his cheeks flushed and eyes wide with terror, was out in front! Bernie had never seen him run so fast!

They arrived at the *Cheese Dip* without a minute to spare. After leaping inside, Crumb slammed down the hatch and shouted for the crew to get the ship under way.

The Mouse Watch training kicked in, the mice working together like a perfectly synchronized clock.

As the frustrated cats reached the end of the dock, the submarine shot through the glass portal that led back out to the open water and sped away into the inky darkness of the ocean.

The glass domes of Catlantis receded in the distance, and Bernie allowed herself a huge sigh of relief.

Glancing around the cabin, she noted that Captain Crumb, Jarvis, and the rest of the crew didn't share her feelings of relief. They managed to escape with the map, but there was one big thing left to worry about. As they plotted the course that would lead to the SS *Moon*, they were all wondering the same thing:

Would they beat the R.A.T.S. to the Milk Saucer? Or would they get to the wreck only to find out that, after all they had gone through, the most dangerous power source in the world had fallen into the hands of evil?

CHAPTER 20

Bubbles flew past the porthole windows as the SS *Cheese Dip* rocketed through the ocean. They reminded Bernie of stars outside a spaceship, just like in *Mouse Trek*. The submarine was going so fast, Bernie knew that there was no way possible for the cats to, well, CAT-ch up.

Cat-ch up. That's a good one. I'll have to tell Jarvis when we've completed the mission, she thought.

It felt wonderful to have a shower and change into a fresh uniform. She felt she could go her entire life without ever smelling fish sauce again!

She glanced at her watch.

One hour and five minutes left.

The engines hummed at full power, and she could feel the vibration through the floor. If it wasn't for the fear of the R.A.T.S. somehow beating them to the SS *Moon*, she would be having the time of her life.

Someday I'd love to go into space, Bernie mused. *To see other planets. Maybe even alien mice! If the moon is made of green cheese, could there be green mice, too? How weird would that be?*

The best part of the trip to the SS *Moon* was that it wasn't as far as Bernie had feared it would be. Crumb had demanded that all engines run at full power, and Bernie was shocked to see how quickly the *Cheese Dip* could move when it needed to. The modifications that Octavia made must have helped, because Crumb looked astonished when he saw how many knots they were traveling.

The entire trip took only twenty nail-biting minutes.

When they got to the location on the map, Bernie and Jarvis were both surprised to see that despite the fact that it had been sunken for so long, the SS *Moon* appeared to be completely intact. The Cold War submarine looked as if it were merely resting on the bottom of the sea next to a craggy cliff. It was a much less modern and sophisticated ship than the SS *Cheese Dip*, but it seemed to have held up surprisingly well.

And knowing that the SS *Moon* possibly held the Milk Saucer, the most powerful secret weapon in the entire world, made Bernie feel awestruck.

"That old ship might still have power," mused Crumb, who, like the others, was staring out the porthole at the sunken vessel. "The batteries should be long dead. But if it's using the Milk Saucer as a power source, there's a chance that it might be keeping the entire ship functioning inside."

"There's no sign of the R.A.T.S. anywhere," said Bernie. "I think we beat them here!"

"I don't know," said Jarvis doubtfully. "The R.A.T.S. are sneaky: they might be already inside. And what are those big, spiky lollipop things floating around the ship?"

Crumb turned away from the porthole with a worried expression. "Those are floating mines, Slinktail. Before we can get close to the SS *Moon*, they'll have to be disarmed. The empress told us that the sub was protected, and Octavia said we should avoid it. Now we know the reason why," he said, sighing.

"Why can't we just swim around them?" asked Bernie.

Crumb shook his head. "The slightest tremor or ripple from someone swimming nearby could set them off. Worse still, because of their size, only a very small mouse can do the disarming. If Slinktail tried to do it, he would cause way too much movement. When you two dive down there, I recommend that he stay back while Bernie goes ahead and disarms them."

He shot Bernie a concerned look. "Your Soggies will show you how to disarm them, but it'll be dangerous. Are you sure you're up to it?"

Bernie had faced elaborate traps before—last time she had found herself stuck in a giant maze—but this felt worse somehow. She was nervous, but even so, not nearly as nervous as she'd been around the cats. This was the kind of danger Bernie welcomed.

"Leave it to me," she said. "And if we're going to finish this mission on time, we have to get in there as quickly as possible. The R.A.T.S. could show up at any minute."

Crumb nodded and then turned to his first mate, saying, "Mr. Fingertwitch, take our two agents to the decompression room and show Agent Skampersky how to access bomb defusing on her Soggies."

Fingertwitch pushed his round glasses back up on his snout and nodded, "Aye, aye, sir!" Bernie and Jarvis followed behind. As they walked, Jarvis put a comforting paw on Bernie's shoulder.

"You can do this, Bern," he said.

Bernie glanced up at him and was surprised to see how calm he was.

"You're not nervous," she commented. Jarvis shrugged.

"I am, actually, but not as much as before. I guess having faced my fears cured me."

Bernie offered a tight smile. It was the first time that she was more nervous than he about going underwater.

Fingertwitch showed Bernie how to access the disarming program in her Soggies menu. Bernie was relieved to see that if she followed the instructions, everything should go off without a hitch.

"Whatever you do, stay calm," said Fingertwitch. "The worst thing you can do is panic and make a sudden move. Those mines are extremely sensitive."

"Got it," said Bernie.

Fingertwitch turned to Jarvis and said, "After she gets them disarmed, then you can follow her inside. Just make sure you hang back and do nothing until then, got it?"

"Aye, aye," said Jarvis.

The first mate sealed up the decompression chamber. As it filled up with water, Bernie and Jarvis secured their goggles.

They swam through the murky water, making their way to the dim outline of the SS *Moon*. They had to go slowly and couldn't use the frog feet since they might detonate the dangerous mines.

When they were about a hundred feet away, Bernie motioned for Jarvis to stay back. The young rat gave her the thumbs-up sign. She could see the worry in his eyes through his glowing green goggles.

"Be careful," Jarvis warned. "I'll watch from up here and keep an eye out for trouble."

"Thanks," said Bernie as she swam away from Jarvis.

Stay calm, she told herself. *No sudden moves. One stroke at a time . . .*

As she approached the first of the huge floating mines, she was struck by the sheer size of it. The long chain that attached it to the seafloor was covered with algae, but the mines themselves must have been made of some kind of rust-resistant metal because they looked as if they were brand-new.

"See anything?" Jarvis's voice crackled through her Soggies.

"Not yet," said Bernie.

She carefully drew close and inspected it. Hardly daring to breathe or even make the smallest bubble, she slowly circled the explosive device, searching for any clue to deactivate it. Her Soggies scanned the mine for any possible way to access a control panel, but she was disappointed when the computerized voice in her ear said, "No information found."

How was that even possible? The goggles were supposed to give her step-by-step instructions on how to disarm the mines!

"My Soggies can't find anything," Bernie said. There was a pause while Jarvis thought about it.

"I'm swimming above them now," said Jarvis. Then

after a moment, he said, "I think there might be something on the top of the mines, like a button maybe. Oh man, wait a minute. . . ."

"What is it?" asked Bernie.

"It's a puzzle," said Jarvis. She could hear the excitement in his voice.

"What is?" asked Bernie.

"There are nine mines surrounding the sub, and they're arranged in three vertical rows. Here, I'll get the Soggies to send you a sketch."

A couple of seconds later, Bernie saw a pattern appear on her display screen. It looked like this:

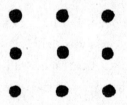

For most mice, that pattern wouldn't have meant much at all. But Bernie had always had very few friends and spent most of her free time studying puzzles. She had been sure that her puzzle-solving skills were what got her recruited to the Mouse Watch, before she learned that it was her bravery instead. Jarvis was even better at puzzles than she was. This one reminded her immediately of a puzzle game that her dad had once taught her.

"Wait! I know that one!" she said excitedly.

"Right?" said Jarvis, sounding equally excited. "I learned that puzzle when I was super little."

"Me too!" said Bernie.

Connect the nine dots using four straight lines without lifting the pencil from the paper.

She knew immediately what she had to do. Swimming over to the mine in the upper right-hand corner, she looked on top of it and was happy to find that there were two buttons positioned there, a red one and a green one.

"There's two buttons on top, one red and one green," Bernie said happily.

"Perfect," said Jarvis.

Green for go, thought Bernie.

She hoped her guess was right.

She proceeded to float above all the mines, gently pushing the green buttons as if she were the pencil drawing four lines and never taking it off the paper.

The end design looked like this.

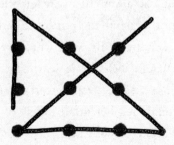

And, sure enough, the moment she pushed the last green button, every single one of the mines suddenly drifted down on their chains until they hit the seafloor bottom, completely disabled.

"Yes!" Bernie shouted.

"Whoo-hoo!" she heard Jarvis cheer through the speaker on her Soggies.

She was so excited that she rushed right up to the submarine door. She wanted nothing more than to be the first one to find the Milk Saucer. It would more than certainly make up for the botched kitten rescue!

Bernie was happy to find that the old submarine's hatch was unlocked and, after rotating the wheel, she entered the decompression chamber.

The water rushed from the well-lit room. Bernie stared around, surprised. As Crumb had surmised, the power was still on, thanks to the Milk Saucer.

If a gadget like that could last this long and continually generate power, it really must be the greatest power source in the world, she thought excitedly.

She pushed the Soggies up on her forehead and stepped over the threshold. Inside, the sub had the same look and feel as the battleship at the docks back at Mouse Watch HQ. The walls were painted an industrial gray-green, like it was military issue.

There wouldn't have been anything very special about

it, if it wasn't for the fact that Bernie knew it held one of the most special objects in the world.

It was the perfect, ordinary shell for hiding an extraordinary pearl.

She glanced down at her watch.

Five minutes left.

She might actually make it!

As she followed the signs down the narrow corridors to the Command Center, a steady heat seemed to emanate from the walls. It confirmed her instincts. The farther she went down the corridor, the brighter the light became until it was so bright she felt the need to lower her Soggies in order to protect her eyes.

"Here we go," she murmured.

Then, taking a deep breath, Bernie turned the corner that led to the main room of the command center and opened the door.

This is it! she thought. *We actually did it. We beat the R.A.T.S. when it counted most!* And then, although she would be ashamed to admit it later, she couldn't help thinking, *Bernie Skampersky, Level One Mouse Watch agent, single-handedly saves the world!*

She strode confidently into the command center, and, just past the main control panel, she saw the treasure she'd been looking for. A small, glowing disk that sat on a simple metal stand. It did actually resemble a milk saucer.

She walked up to it, feeling awestruck. On the floor by the stand was a black box that was exactly the size and shape of the Milk Saucer and a pair of big, mouse-size metal tongs.

Bernie used the tongs to carefully lift the Milk Saucer and place it in the box. Her heart swelled as she shut the lid and latched it tight.

With her heart soaring in her chest, she reached down and hit the "Stop" button on her watch. At one minute, fifty-eight seconds, the little figure froze in place. She knew that a transmission would be sent wirelessly back to Mouse Watch HQ, announcing that the mission was accomplished.

She had the Milk Saucer and had beaten the R.A.T.S.

It was the best feeling in the whole world!

As she turned to exit the room, feeling triumphant and ready to return heroically to the SS *Cheese Dip*, she stopped short.

Her blood ran cold.

A row of leering rats holding sharp-looking crochet hooks and knitting needles stood between Bernie and the door. One of them, a tall female wearing a puffy vest, looked anxious and uncomfortable, but Bernie didn't have time to figure out why. She was too horrified by the old crone holding Jarvis by the throat.

He'd been caught!

Bernie felt the Milk Saucer slide from her grip and clatter to the floor. The old crone saw it and, with a horrible grin, said, "Well, well, well, there's no use crying over spilled milk."

CHAPTER 21

"Let him go," Bernie said through gritted teeth.

The old rat crone cackled and squeezed Jarvis's throat harder, making him squeal. "You led us here, dearie. But WE were smart enough to avoid the cat city. Abiatha wonders, what on earth were you thinking? Little mouse with little brains. First Abiatha gets to squeeze this one and then she squeezes you, my dearie. Makes Kryptos proud, she will. Abiatha Squint always gets her targets and now she gets the Milk Saucer as a bonus!"

There's that name again, Bernie thought. *Kryptos.*

So, the R.A.T.S. had been following them to get her and Jarvis. They didn't know about the Milk Saucer, but now, seeing it firsthand, they were going to take it for themselves. She wondered if this group knew that Octavia wanted it, too.

"Why do you want us?" asked Bernie. "What did we ever do to you?"

"You embarrassed him," said a meek voice. Bernie saw that it was the awkward-looking female rat with the puffy vest. "Kryptos doesn't like to be humiliated. He wants both of your lives so he can send a message that he's still in control."

Bernie made a mental note. *So, Kryptos is their leader! Is Octavia working for him?*

"Well, whoever he is, he can't. I won't let him or any-body else!" Bernie balled up her fists, trying desperately to figure a way out of this. "Now let him go!"

"No," croaked Abiatha Squint. "I won't. Give us the saucer, dearie, or I kills him right now." Jarvis stared back at her, terrified. The scraggly old rat seemed possessed. She began squeezing tighter until Jarvis's cheeks turned blue.

The struggle inside Bernie's heart at that moment was the most powerful she'd ever felt. There was no question about how much she loved her friend, but she also knew that if she let the R.A.T.S. have the Milk Saucer, they would destroy not only her and Jarvis, but also the entire world!

It was an impossible decision.

But then, one other option presented itself to Bernie. Why did it only have to be either choice A or choice B?

Why not choose C?

With a berserker scream, Bernie launched the Orca directly at Abiatha Squint. The old crone was taken aback by the gigantic killer whale suddenly careening toward her. She screeched and ducked, releasing her grip on Jarvis. As Squint released her grip, several things happened at once. Jarvis kicked out at her as hard as he could. Bernie knew that he was a terrible fighter, but when his life was on the line, he used every bit of strength that he had.

In every self-defense training test, Jarvis had come in last. But his teacher at HQ would have been incredibly proud to see that, for once in his life, he executed a perfect roundhouse kick, connecting with the side of the old crone's wrinkly jaw. Abiatha cursed and staggered backward.

Bernie launched herself at the nearest rat and sank her teeth into his leg, biting down as hard as she could.

"AAAAH!" the rat screamed.

The attack took all the rats by surprise. Jarvis wriggled and squirmed away from the other rats that tried to grab him and finally managed to kick another one in the shin. Bernie used every fighting technique she possessed—paw, tail, and teeth! She was a furry tornado, causing chaos as she lashed out in every direction. She hardly felt the Milk Saucer slip from her grip as she aimed a karate chop at a lunging opponent.

The R.A.T.S. hadn't expected such resistance from their young targets. They fought with desperation, but Jarvis and

Bernie weren't going to go down easily even though they were outnumbered.

Abiatha Squint rose from the ground, snarling. Her gaze was filled with red-hot fury, and the howl that came from her throat stunned everyone, stopping the chaotic fight like a freeze ray.

"NOBODY ESCAPES ABIATHA SQUINT!" she screamed, and launched herself directly at Bernie. The young mouse was caught completely off guard, terror freezing every one of her limbs as the snarling crone flew directly at her.

This is it.

She squeezed her eyes shut.

But then there was a bright flash of light and a very loud *CLANG!*

Abiatha Squint crumpled halfway through her midair jump, falling to the ground in a heap. Standing shakily next to her was the anxious-looking rat, holding the Milk Saucer above her head. She'd smashed the glowing disk directly onto Abiatha Squint's head, knocking the formidable rat unconscious.

Nobody said a word. The other R.A.T.S. agents were frozen. They didn't know what to do. The leader of the mission had just taken out one of the most formidable assassins in the R.A.T.S. army. That had never happened before!

Jarvis and the nervous-looking rat in the Hawaiian shirt and puffy vest exchanged a long, searching look.

"Juno? Is that you?" asked Jarvis.

"RUN!" she shouted, pushing Jarvis toward the confused Bernie.

"STOP THEM!" shouted the largest of the R.A.T.S. soldiers.

Juno stepped between the rats and the fleeing Watchers.

As a clattering commotion erupted behind them, Bernie and Jarvis raced down the hallway that led to the decompression chamber. Soon they heard the pounding footsteps of the guards that had gotten past Juno racing behind them.

There was no time to hesitate. They had to run as fast as they possibly could if they were going to make it.

The door to the decompression chamber was ten feet away.

Then it was five.

Finally, with the guards practically breathing down their necks, Bernie and Jarvis dove inside the chamber and slammed the iron door, locking the guards out.

With rat fists pounding on the door behind them, Bernie quickly pressed the button that filled the room with seawater. Then, after a few excruciating seconds, the exit door finally swung open and, without a moment to lose, the two Watchers engaged their frog feet and sped away toward the SS *Cheese Dip*.

Their fins churned up the water like a pair of electric mixers.

Suddenly, out of the darkness, an ominous shape appeared. It grew bigger and bigger, dwarfing the mice as they stared up at it in disbelief. The *Medusa*! Octavia had arrived.

But this time, they knew the captain wasn't there to rescue them. The two mice watched as the eight tentacles reached toward the SS *Moon* and pried it loose from the seafloor where it had rested for decades, releasing a cloud of dust and debris.

Bernie and Jarvis watched helplessly, tiny specks in a massive ocean, as the kraken towed its prize back to Catlantis. Octavia would finish the bargain she'd made with the empress, bringing her a bunch of new furry morsels and getting a new sub to keep as her own.

Although they'd escaped with their lives, Bernie and Jarvis had failed in their mission.

Octavia had the Milk Saucer and the empress would get the nice plump rats for dinner.

Octavia the traitor.

The thought of her made Bernie sick.

They didn't have the Milk Saucer, and the SS *Moon*

was gone. All that was left was a ragged hole in the ocean floor. Bernie couldn't help thinking, as she floated there in the vast, silent ocean, that one day it would be overgrown with sea life and nobody would ever know how they'd tried to save the world from destruction.

But it was too late.

"Well, there goes the Milk Saucer," said Bernie sadly.

"You mean here *comes* the Milk Saucer," Jarvis replied over his Soggies' radio.

"What?" Bernie glanced over at him. With a triumphant grin, Jarvis pulled the glowing disk from his hoodie. Bernie stared, mouth agape. "How?"

"We did it," said Jarvis.

Bernie grinned at him. "No, you did it, Jarvie! You got the Milk Saucer!"

"No. WE did it, Bernie. You rescued me from Squint. I got the Milk Saucer from Juno. Unlike Octavia, we always work as a team. That's why we're in the Mouse Watch and she isn't."

Bernie knew that he was 100 percent right. Even though she used to love her independence, the idea of ending up like Octavia wasn't the least bit interesting anymore. She loved being part of a team . . . especially with Jarvis as her teammate.

If they hadn't been floating in the middle of the ocean, she would have rushed over and given him the biggest hug of his life. Instead, grinning widely, she motioned for Jarvis to start swimming.

"Let's get that thing back to the *Cheese Dip* as soon as possible! I don't want to stay out here in the middle of the ocean a minute longer than we have to."

And even though he didn't say it, Bernie knew that Jarvis couldn't have agreed more.

ernie and Jarvis proudly presented the black box containing the Milk Saucer to Gadget Hackwrench. Captain Crumb stood next to her, beaming down at the young agents. He was dressed in his finest sea captain's coat and hat and looked happier than Bernie had ever seen him.

Gadget received the box, holding it carefully with two hands. She grinned back at both of them.

"You've both earned an advancement to Level Two and special medals of commendation for courage in unusual circumstances," she said. "And although it wasn't quite mission accomplished when you stopped your watch, Bernie, I think a few bonus minutes are okay. After all, you both did something that was incredibly brave and nearly impossible."

"Thank you, ma'am," they replied in unison.

An explosion of applause echoed in the Mouse Watch assembly room. Bernie blushed, feeling happy and honored.

"And you should also know that Captain Crumb here has spoken very highly of you both. It wasn't long after we were deployed to London that we discovered that it was a tactic by the R.A.T.S. to divert us. We think whoever their mysterious leader is knew exactly what they were doing. They were bent on eliminating two of the best young recruits the Mouse Watch has had in ages. Thankfully, you were able to stop them from getting both you and the Milk Saucer."

"Just doing our jobs, ma'am," said Bernie and Jarvis together.

"Their leader's name is Kryptos and he must be stopped," called a voice from the back of the room. The crowd turned to see a new rat walking forward, a determined expression on her face.

Jarvis beamed at the smiling rat. "Juno? How did you . . ."

"Octavia delivered the SS *Moon* to Catlantis. She was livid when she found that the Milk Saucer wasn't on it. The last I saw, Octavia was running through the city trying to avoid the guards the empress had sent after her. The big cat was eager to have every rat she could get her hands on for what she called a welcome feast, and I guess she decided Octavia looked too juicy to pass up. Fortunately for me, they were so busy chasing her that I was able to slip away in one of the *Medusa*'s escape pods."

Bernie stared at her, impressed. There was much more to Juno than at first glance. She definitely seemed like a rat worth getting to know!

"Because she exhibited such bravery, helping to save two agents' lives, we've decided to welcome Juno to the Mouse Watch," said Gadget. "She says she has a lot of details about our enemies that she wants to share."

"You bet I do!" agreed Juno.

More cheers erupted in the big room, practically lifting the roof from the walls. Bernie felt happy for the bedraggled-looking rat. She was grinning widely and looked incredibly grateful to be somewhere where rodents were nice for a change!

As the crowd dispersed from the leveling-up ceremony, Jarvis turned to Bernie and asked, "Wanna play Mice and Dice?"

"What's that?" asked Bernie.

"Come on, Juno and I will show you. It's only the best game on the planet!"

The three were about to walk down from the platform when Gadget stopped them short. "Wait, I only have one question," said Gadget.

"What's that?" asked Bernie.

"What's all this I keep hearing about Tabasco sauce?"

she asked, glancing at Jarvis. "I've never tried it; is it good?"

Jarvis reached into his pocket and was about to hand it over when Bernie stopped him. "No, no, no, ma'am. You'll get as addicted as he is!"

Their laughter was interrupted by a Mouse Watch agent wearing a tweed vest and bow tie, who dashed into the gleaming conference room looking red-faced and out of breath.

"What is it, Walter?"

"A call from Catlantis, ma'am," said Walter Gouda, mopping his brow with a handkerchief. "The empress is onscreen now," he added.

Gadget pressed a button on the conference room table, and a large screen rose from inside it. Bernie and Jarvis stared, feeling uncomfortable, at the Grand Tabby herself.

Bernie flinched and looked away. It was hard to look someone in the eye who had tried to eat you.

"Hello," said Gadget coldly.

"Grrrreetings," purred the empress. "I just wanted to call to make surrre you know that we didn't mean anything malicious by attempting to have your agents for dinner. You might say that it's our animal instinct to find your species . . . well, rrrather scrrrrumptious-looking."

"We don't take getting eaten lightly. We're apt to resist," said Gadget firmly but diplomatically.

The cat chuckled, sending her rolls of chubby, furry

flesh rippling. "We are satisfied to keep all Mouse Watch agents off the menu from now on. We prefurrr the taste of rats. They were a real delicacy."

Her eyes darted to Bernie and Jarvis. "And thank you again for rescuing Bubbles. Kittens are young and inexperienced. Sometimes they get themselves in over their heads."

She smiled at Bernie and Jarvis, and Bernie could detect nothing but kindness in it.

"But one should also neverrrrr underestimate the young. Sometimes, they can surprise you with theirrrr courage."

Bernie knew that the compliment was directed at her and Jarvis, and she grinned. *Maybe some cats aren't so bad*, she thought.

"I will communicate with the cats on the surrrface," continued the empress. "From now on, any members of the Mouse Watch and their families need only invoke my name and they shall have our prrrrrotection."

With that, the empress gave a slight nod of her regal head and the screen winked out.

Bernie stared thoughtfully at the darkened screen for a long moment.

"Wait until I tell Mom and Dad that they never have to worry about a cat attack again," she said, finally, to Jarvis. "They'll never believe it."

EPILOGUE

Kryptos paced up and down the richly embroidered carpet in his sumptuous, yet impeccably organized, office. He was tired of trusting incompetent underlings to achieve his goals. This time, he had to work harder than usual to hide the fury that was raging inside him.

"This is completely unacceptable," he murmured. He fidgeted with his tie, trying to keep his double Windsor knot completely even as he stared into a mirror.

He'd had both a plan and a backup, and each one had failed. Octavia was supposed to retrieve the Milk Saucer. Juno was supposed to track and eliminate the young Mouse Watch agents, ensuring that they would never be a problem again.

It was foolproof.

Only it hadn't been.

Octavia's failure was completely unexpected. Juno was barely competent, but with Squint at her side he'd thought it was a decent fail-safe. She'd not only failed but had also turned traitor. The Milk Saucer was critical to his plans and, once again, the two young Mouse Watch agents had gotten in the way.

"Skampersky and Slinktail," murmured Kryptos. "You have made a fool of me for the last time."

He turned to his assistant, just the latest in a long line of interchangeable assistants. The rat wore a tidy blue button-down shirt and neatly pressed khaki pants. His shoes shined. Kryptos preferred shiny shoes.

In a low, dangerous voice, Kryptos said, "No more hiding. I want you to send a message to every single R.A.T.S. operative at every one of our bases worldwide. Inform them that our days of sneaking around are over. We are officially at war with the Mouse Watch. Let them know that I, Kryptos, will no longer hide in the shadows. I will lead the attack."

He clenched his fist so tightly that his knuckles turned white. Turning back, he gazed into the mirror and whispered, "It's time for me to show my face to the world."

ACKNOWLEDGMENTS

I'd like to express my profound gratitude to my editor, Jocelyn Davies, and her talented bunch of Level Ten Watcher Agents at Disney Hyperion. You guys are the reason these books are so much fun to write.

I'd also like to thank my youngest daughter, Olivia. She's a very talented puzzle-solver and the real inspiration for Bernie Skampersky. This series, and all its cheesy jokes, is dedicated to your beautiful, creative spirit.

Turn the page for a sneak peek at the
Mouse Watch's next adventure!

CHAPTER 1

"Top Secret? Isn't everything we do here considered top secret?" Bernie Skampersky asked.

The little mouse's haystack of blue-dyed hair flew back over her head as she hurried past a row of glass-enclosed cubicles in the sprawling, hi-tech Mouse Watch facility. Her best friend Jarvis loped alongside her, huffing and puffing as he tried to keep pace.

They passed a glass-enclosed office with a row of harried looking agents holding digital tablets. The hipster techies were punching away at virtual keyboards and arguing about the best encryption software. Bernie knew that security at Mouse Watch HQ had long been a priority for the organization. The foul rodents of R.A.T.S. were always looking for a way to hack into their databases and servers.

It seemed like whatever the Mouse Watch did to make

the world a safer place, there was an enemy trying to undo it.

Just part of the job, Bernie reminded herself.

The twisting hallways were brightly lit with LED lights that dimmed behind them as the agents dashed down the hall. When Bernie was a new recruit, it seemed to take her forever to get anywhere—the curved halls wound through the building in a dizzying pattern that often confused her. But now that she was a Level One agent, she was a solid pro and knew exactly, right down to the second, how much time it would take to get to Conference Room A.

"Bernie, (huff, huff) this is an ALL HANDS meeting," Jarvis said, trying to catch his breath. "In all the time . . . that we've been here . . . that's never, (puff) happened."

"That's true," admitted Bernie as she zipped around a drone station filled with flying surveillance robots. "We've got over a thousand agents now! How are they going to pack everybody into one room?"

Jarvis's mop of blond hair flopped comically from beneath his hoodie as he ran, sweat pouring down his forehead. "Hold on a sec, Bernie, would ya? Why do you always want to run? I have a cramp."

Jarvis leaned against a desk, gasping. Bernie danced impatiently in place, glancing at the countdown timer on her smartwatch. She was anxious to get to the meeting. Her black Level Two agent's jumpsuit was sleek and cool. Her smart goggles and watch were activated, and both of them glowed with a steady, blue light. When the little mouse caught sight of her reflection in one of the glass walls, she liked what she saw. All of her working out was paying off. Her speed had increased so much that having a last name like "Skampersky" finally did her justice.

She was becoming every bit the Mouse Watch agent she'd dreamed of becoming since she was little.

"Just like Gadget," she murmured happily. Gadget Hackwrench was her hero and the leader of the Mouse Watch. The aging inventor had been an inspiration to her from the time Bernie first heard about her adventures with the Rescue Rangers as a mouseling. It was a dream come true for her to get to work with the legendary founder of the Watch.

"Hey, Jarvie, I wonder if Chip and Dale will be there. I still can't believe they actually, personally assigned us to our last top secret mission."

"Don't remind me! And I certainly hope they're not here," groused Jarvis. "Going back underwater doesn't sound fun to me at all."

"But you said you were okay with it," said Bernie. "After we rescued the Milk Saucer, you said that you were getting over your fear of water."

Jarvis gave her a withering stare. "Being just *okay* with

something doesn't mean that I'm itching to do it again any time soon." He mopped his forehead with the back of his hoodie sleeve. "I don't care if I ever set foot in a submarine again."

Bernie thought back to their last adventure, reveling in the danger and excitement that they'd experienced deep under the ocean.

She and Jarvis had been assigned duties on the SS *Cheese Dip*, a top secret submarine. They had raced against the clock to retrieve the Million Kilowatt Generator—nicknamed the "Milk Saucer"—from a sunken Cold War era submarine called the SS *Moon*. It was an unlimited power device, a secret weapon, one that had been thought lost to history. The mission had been filled with all kinds of things that she'd imagined a top level Mouse Watch agent would face. She'd seen incredible sea creatures in a stunning underwater setting, visited a mysterious underwater city populated with cats, and had also rescued the most powerful weapon that the Mouse Watch had ever found.

The *Milk Saucer* could have been used to destroy the entire world if it had fallen into the wrong hands.

But thankfully, Bernie and Jarvis had saved the day.

Bernie grinned, thinking about how she and Jarvis had survived so many things. For a second or two, she hadn't been entirely sure that they would escape that mission with their lives (and tails) intact. But they had, and they'd done it together. Rather than scare her off, the danger had only made Bernie crave the next big adventure.

Bernie glanced at Jarvis, who had caught his breath and was now eating a hunk of cheddar cheese he'd been carrying in his pocket. She watched as he drenched it with Tabasco sauce from a minibottle he'd been keeping in his other pocket, and took a huge bite.

"Seriously! You're eating again? We've got a meeting to get to!"

Jarvis nodded with his mouth full and said in a garbled voice, "Gotta keep . . . *mmf* . . . my strength up."

A cheery voice from behind them caused Bernie to look up. Among the throngs of mouse agents making their way to the meeting was a tall rat with big, green eyes and a snaggletooth that stuck out from below her upper lip. She waved excitedly when she made eye contact with Bernie and rushed over, beaming with excitement.

"Bernie!" The rat threw her arms around Bernie in a crushing hug.

"H-Hi, Juno!" squeaked Bernie in reply. No sooner had Juno released her grip on Bernie than she had Jarvis crushed in an equally fierce embrace.

"Hi, Jarvie!" she exclaimed.

"Whoa! Okay!" Jarvis grunted, choking down his bite of cheese. "I can't believe the nickname *Jarvie* is sticking. B, you're a bad influence!"

"I think it's cute!" Juno said happily.

"You look great, Juno!" Bernie exclaimed.

Bernie had first met Juno during their last adventure, when the rat had turned on her evil bosses and helped Bernie and Jarvis escape. At that time, she'd been a depressed, ragged-looking thing. But Juno had undergone a complete transformation since defecting from the R.A.T.S. Her eyes sparkled, her fur was neatly brushed and clean, and she wore a bright yellow Level One jumpsuit. The rat had often mentioned how much she loved Bernie's blue hair and had, at Bernie's encouragement, dyed her own a bright, electric pink, which she now wore in a spiky, punk rock style.

After a few months at the Mouse Watch, she was a whole new rat.

"Omigosh, did you guys have any of those AMAZING pancakes they had in the cafeteria this morning? I've never tasted anything so good!" Juno exclaimed.

Bernie gave her a puzzled glance. "They were just normal pancakes. . . ."

"Maybe a little better than average with Tabasco sauce," added Jarvis, waggling his half-empty bottle.

"Are you kidding me? They were delicious! And that dollop of creamy ricotta cheese, pistachios, and honey on the side was unbelievable. My mouth still waters just thinking of it!" said Juno, looking shocked. "You guys don't understand. Back at the R.A.T.S. base we had nothing but gray soup for every meal!"

"Gray soup? What's *gray soup?*" asked Bernie.

Juno made a gagging motion with her paw and said, "Nobody knows. Most of us think it was the dirty water left over from washing old socks in the rusted washing machines."

"EEEWWW," said Bernie and Jarvis in chorus.

"Right!" agreed Juno. She stretched her arms wide, indicating the entire Mouse Watch facility. "This is heaven! I can have baths whenever I want! There's good food, great friends, and nobody ever calls me names. I've never been so happy!"

Bernie felt a surge of compassion for her new friend. Jarvis had told her everything he'd gone through before they met, and how hard life could be for rats. But hearing it again from Juno only reminded Bernie how grateful she herself should be.

A chime sounded on Bernie's smartwatch. Looking down, she saw the running, cartoon version of herself, and next to it, a text that read, MEETING BEGINS IN TWO MINUTES.

"Guys, we gotta hurry!" said Bernie.

"Why is everything *hurry* with you these days?" grumbled Jarvis. "Whatever happened to leisurely walks? Or, better yet, getting electric scooters that can take walking out of the equation entirely! I need to mention that idea to Gadget. . . ."

Bernie and Juno half-dragged, half-pushed a protesting Jarvis the rest of the way to Conference Room A. They ended up being the last to enter with just a few seconds to spare. Once inside, Bernie gazed around. Jarvis was right, it was as big as a stadium! Rows and rows of seats, enough to house the entire California division of the Mouse Watch, stretched from floor to ceiling. The place was practically filled to capacity and Bernie was glad when Jarvis spotted a row of three seats together near the stage.

As they sat down and settled in for the meeting, Bernie lowered her Mouse Watch goggles so that she could see the stage in enhanced reality. The goggles she wore weren't the standard issue. These were SeaGogs, nick-named "Soggies" by the crew that served on the SS *Cheese Dip*. Her original pair, unfortunately, had been stolen by Captain Octavia on the underwater mission, and she wished she still had them.

I won't let her get away with that. Someday, I'll get them back.

Her thoughts of revenge were interrupted as the lights dimmed. A spotlight flared. Then, applause filled the massive room as Gadget Hackwrench appeared from behind a flowing, golden curtain. She wore her usual lavender cov-eralls and her graying hair was cut in a neatly coiffed bob.

Like the other agents, she wore a pair of enhanced reality goggles perched on her forehead.

She waved at the huge crowd with excitement dancing in her eyes.

"Greetings, Watchers!" said Gadget. "Thank you all for coming. I'm excited to say that today is definitely a day we'll all remember. I'm very proud to present what I think is my greatest invention to date." A hush of anticipation filled the room. Bernie could hardly sit still. Her mind raced, thinking about all the incredible things Gadget could make.

I'll bet it's something amazing, she thought. After all, why the big meeting if it wasn't going to be spectacular?

"I'm thinking it's a time machine," whispered Jarvis.

"What?" Bernie hissed back.

"A TIME MACHINE! Wouldn't that be cool?" asked Jarvis. "If I had one, I would go back to the Old West and meet my hero, Tobasco Johnson. He was the gunslinger who invented the sauce that makes life worth living."

"I think that's impossible, even for Gadget. You've been streaming too much sci-fi on MouseTube," said Bernie.

"You can never have too much sci-fi," said Jarvis seriously. "I just completed an amazing series on alien abductions. B, you totally should watch it."

"No, thank you," said Bernie, grimacing. "I hate that stuff. Creeps me out."

"Are you kidding me right now? Science fiction is the best!" Jarvis appeared to be settling in for a debate when Juno elbowed him to be quiet. Gadget continued her speech.

"Ladies and Gentlemice, allow me to introduce to you a very special someone. It's someone that can be several places at once. Someone who knows more information than ten thousand encyclopedias and all the professors of all the colleges in the world put together. This someone will be your best friend and the R.A.T.S. worst enemy. Mouse Watch agents, please give a warm round of applause for . . . TONY!"

CHAPTER 2

"Hi, everybody! I can't tell you how excited I am to be working with you!"

Every jaw in the stadium dropped as a friendly, disembodied voice filled the room. Bernie wondered what was going on. Was there someone hiding backstage with a microphone? *What's the big deal?* she wondered. She glanced around, puzzled at the response.

Gadget noticed all the puzzled looks and chuckled. "No, you won't see Tony walking around. Tony is our new, state-of-the-art Artificial Intelligence agent that will be helping to *catapult the Mouse Watch into the future!*"

No way! That's so cool!

The voice sounded incredibly real, and had a casual tone that was like listening to an old friend who had stopped by for a visit. Bernie had heard A.I. voices before on smartphones, but this one was very different. Tony actually sounded like a real mouse, and it was hard to believe that the voice didn't have a physical body to go with it.

"That's right, agents, with the help of Tony's vast database, we'll be able to take our mission to save the world to a whole new level!" said Gadget.

Polite applause.

"TONY stands for Tailored Omnipresent Nice guY," Gadget continued. She shrugged sheepishly and added, "I know, I know. . . . The acronym is a bit of a stretch using the "Y" on the end of "guy." But TONG sounded too much like a salad server and he's so much more than that."

Polite giggles.

Gadget, grinning at the crowd, continued her speech. "Tony will customize himself to your personal needs and is there for you when you're in a pinch. He will never let you down."

Scattered applause filled the vast chamber. It was evident that many of the agents were still feeling a bit confused as to what exactly Tony did or where he was. Gadget could see the mystified expressions on a lot of the agent's faces and motioned for silence. "I know it's a lot to take in. The Tony system will be integrated into our new fleet of drones, enabling them to navigate obstacles and make split-second decisions that could save our pilots from danger." Gadget directed her voice skyward. "Hey, Tony, would you mind describing for everyone what sorts of other ways you could help on a mission?"

The Tony program chuckled, and the system's voice echoed around the room as it replied, "Sure thing, Gadg."

Gadg? thought Bernie. *I've never heard anyone call her that.* Gadget was very nice, but she was also such a great leader. Everyone respected her so much that Bernie couldn't imagine being so informal with her.

"Let's see, well, the first thing to know about me is that I never sleep and I don't eat . . . *much*," Tony joked. A few mice giggled, breaking the stunned silence.

"That's good," whispered Jarvis, grinning. "I don't need the competition."

"Pay attention!" hissed Juno.

Tony continued, saying, "The truth is, I cater my database toward the individual needs of the agent I'm interacting with. You'll find that I'm a friend you can count on and that I'll get to know you better the more you ask me for help. I learn from you and you can learn from me. Isn't that great?"

Gadget nodded and gestured toward the crowd. "Beneath your chairs you'll each find a small case. Please reach down and open them now."

Feeling puzzled but excited, Bernie felt around beneath her chair and pulled out a small, plain-looking black box.

She lifted the silver buckle that kept the lid fastened shut. Then, after opening the top of the case, Bernie's heart skipped a beat.

"New goggles!" she exclaimed happily. These new ones looked so cool, she almost forgot her grudge against Octavia for stealing her old ones. The specs had sweeping black and chrome sides and a tiny Mouse Watch logo, the iconic "MW" gear, engraved between the lenses.

She immediately put the sleek device over her eyes. As soon as the goggles booted up, Tony's voice sounded loud and clear, as if he were sitting directly on her shoulder.

"Hi, Bernie Skampersky! Nice to meet you! How are you doing?"

By some high-tech wizardry, Gadget had managed to have the A.I. voice conduct directly from the goggle's contact point at her temple into her head without any kind of special attachment or earpiece.

"Wow!" whispered Bernie, startled at how realistic the effect was. She'd had no idea how the system had recognized her by name, but judging by the gasps of delight around the room, all the other agents were experiencing the same thing.

"Well? Cat got your tongue?" asked Tony.

"C-c-cat? What cat?" asked Bernie nervously.

"Oh, that's right, you've been to Catlantis. Bad joke. Seriously, I've really looked forward to meeting you. I've scanned all your records and I have to say, I am *quite* a fan!" said Tony.

Bernie blushed. Although Tony was just a computer program, it sounded so real that she couldn't help feeling flattered by the compliment.

"Um, thanks," said Bernie. "I really don't know what to say. Am I supposed to ask you to do something?"

"You can if you want to. Or, if your mind's a blank, I could show you how to work your new goggles. I really think they're the most impressive thing Gadget has ever come up with."

"Now that's saying a lot," whispered Bernie.

"I agree!" said Tony. "And she also invented *me*, so that's REALLY saying a lot."

Bernie laughed. Juno, who was sitting on Bernie's left, leaned over. Bernie noticed that she was wearing her goggles and had a look of stunned amazement on her furry face.

"Do we really get to keep these?" Juno asked, awestruck.

Bernie nodded. Juno looked so excited she could have fainted on the spot. "This . . . is . . . the . . . greatest . . . day . . . of . . . my . . . life!" she exclaimed.

Tony's voice sounded in Bernie's ear. "Hey, let me show you something real quick. You'll love it. Okay, so when you think about the best day you've ever had, what comes to mind?"

Bernie's mind flashed back on a particular day she'd

spent with Jarvis. "Well, once Jarvis and I had ice cream at this great little shop in Santa Barbara. We took the train up there on a Saturday when we didn't have any Watcher duties. . . ."

". . . Okay, let me stop you right there," interrupted Tony. "Let me check my database. Oh, got it. You had peppermint candy ice cream, right?"

"Yes! But how could you possibly know that?"

Tony laughed. "I cross-referenced all the ice cream shops in Santa Barbara, found security camera footage of every Saturday in the last year, face mapped every visitor, and found a recording of you and Jarvis. Simple."

It certainly didn't sound simple to Bernie. Tony was faster than the fastest computer she'd ever used.

"Okay now, sit back and close your eyes. Relax."

Bernie automatically did as she was told.

"The temperature that day was seventy-four degrees Fahrenheit," Tony said. "There was a light breeze out of the west, carrying with it the scent of the beach and a nearby hot dog cart. . . ."

Bernie felt a warm breeze tickle the fur on her face and arms, carrying with it the delicious scent she remembered. Even though she *knew* she was inside a crowded stadium, she *felt* like she was there, in Santa Barbara, breathing in the fresh air.

"How did you do that?" Bernie asked, amazed.

"Never mind," Tony chuckled. "Way too complicated to explain advanced neural haptics right now. Okay, you should be feeling a spoon in your right paw right . . . NOW. Do you feel it?"

Bernie grinned and nodded as her paw closed around what felt like a plastic spoon. "Wow!"

"Okay," Tony whispered. "Now, with your eyes closed, dip that spoon into the peppermint ice cream you imagine sitting right in front of you and take a bite."

Bernie obeyed. To her utter amazement, she felt the cool, creamy texture of McCornell's peppermint crunch ice cream on her tongue. She swallowed, and it felt like she'd eaten some even though it wasn't there.

"AMAZING!" Bernie cried.

"*Amazing* is what I do," said Tony proudly. "And that's just for fun. Imagine if you needed to process an environment prior to doing a mission? You would know exactly what the conditions felt like and what you were up against."

Bernie opened her eyes and shook her head in amazement. It seemed like just when she thought she'd seen the best of what Gadget could do, her mentor always surprised her.

The entire stadium filled with a rising commotion of "oohs" and "aahs" as Tony led the other Watchers through similar experiences. After a few seconds, Gadget motioned for silence and all eyes were once again riveted back upon her. This time, every agent in the assembly could see the incredible possibilities for what Gadget had created. The hushed crowd was as attentive as if they were at a magic show and Merlin himself was performing.

"So, as you can see, Tony has many uses," Gadget said. "But the system is just the beginning. Tony is critical to the next phase of Mouse Watch security."

Behind Gadget, a projector flickered on, and a three-dimensional, holographic display of a metal sphere with long antennae coming out of it appeared. It rotated slowly and majestically on the stage.

"Thanks to the recovery of the *Milk Saucer* by agents Jarvis Slinktail and Bernadette Skampersky, we are about to launch a brand-new, top secret satellite into space." Gadget gestured to the hologram. "The goal of this satellite is to use the *Milk Saucer*'s powerful, endless energy source to save the planet. Ladies and gentlemice, with this new invention we will create a bubble around the Earth that will halt, and reverse, the effects of global warming permanently."

Excited gasps filled the room. Bernie could hardly believe her ears! What Gadget was proposing could save millions of lives, many more than the Mouse Watch had ever saved in its entire history! It was staggering! It was stupendous!

"And this mission to space," Gadget continued as

the thunderous applause died down, "will be conducted by none other than our two up-and-coming stars in the Watch. Jarvis Slinktail and Bernadette Skampersky, would you please stand up?"

Bernie thought she had fur in her ears. With stunned looks on both of their faces, she and Jarvis rose shakily to their feet. In a billion years Bernie would have never guessed that this would be happening. She was over-whelmed by the waves of raucous applause that once again erupted across the room.

Gadget grinned and motioned for quiet. "These young agents have impressed us all with their courage and unique talents. I feel certain that they're up to the task of going where no mouse has gone before—outer space."

Another round of cheers echoed through the big audi-torium. Juno banged her paws together so hard that her goggles nearly fell off. Bernie's mind was reeling. She saw Jarvis out of the corner of her eye and was shocked to see that rather than the usual, sick look of fear that the news of a new mission had produced in the past, he was grinning ecstatically.

"I *knew* watching sci-fi movies would pay off!" he shouted.

Up until that moment, Bernie had believed that there was no danger she wouldn't have loved to face. She'd even been hoping for more! But with the terrifying reality that she was going to be rocketed into space, Bernie felt more than just weak in the knees.

The agents exited the assembly, placing their old goggles into the provided recycling bins and donning their exciting new ones. Bernie's mouth was dry and her paws shook as she endured the steady stream of congratulations, handshakes, and good-natured shoulder squeezes.

"Hey, Bernie, are you okay?" asked Jarvis, noticing for the first time how pale she'd gotten.

Bernie couldn't find the words to reply. For an answer, she ran as fast as she could to the nearest bathroom and completely lost the pancake breakfast that Juno had been raving about just a few minutes before.